With Warm Regards
Deane C Davis

Nothin' But the Truth

Nothin' But the Truth

More Yankee Yarns

Deane C. Davis

Illustrated by Sue Storey

The New England Press
Shelburne, Vermont

The New England Press, Inc.
P.O. Box 525
Shelburne, Vermont 05482

Library of Congress Catalog Card Number: 82-80343
ISBN: 0-933050-10-0

Newlin B. Wildes's story "The Jumping Horse" first appeared in *Flying Your Way* and is reprinted here with the permission of the author.

Introduction

Brian Vachon

It was nearly ten years ago that I had my first encounter with the author of this book. I had very recently moved from midtown Manhattan to midtown Montpelier to become editor of the state-owned magazine, *Vermont Life*. Toward the end of my first week on the job, my secretary came into my office and told me that the Governor was on the telephone.

"The Governor's office?" I asked.

"The *Governor*," she said.

There followed a moment that I was neither prepared for nor able to face with anything approximating grace under pressure. I had never met Deane C. Davis but during my very short stay in Vermont, I had certainly heard about him. The gifted trial lawyer who became a Vermont Superior Court judge at the tender age of thirty one. The man who subsequently became general counsel and then president and ultimately board chairman and chief executive officer of National Life Insurance Company of Vermont. The man who, at age sixty eight, upon retiring from the insurance business — at an age when most people retire, period — ran for governor of Vermont and was elected. He ran two years later and was elected again and his accomplishments as the state's chief executive officer were considerable. And now he was on the telephone waiting to talk with me. What could he possibly want? Was he upset that a New Yorker had been named editor of Vermont's own magazine? Was he going to make sure he had an influence over my editorial policy? Was he going to fire me?

I cleared my throat and picked up the phone.

"Brian, this is Deane Davis," he said. There was a reassuring sound to his voice.

"Yes Governor. Good afternoon. I hope I didn't keep you waiting."

"Not at all. Look Brian, I'd like to get together with you soon. Maybe over lunch. But I thought I ought to call this afternoon. There's a kind of nasty storm moving up our way and I think you should let your staff leave early today. No sense in us all worrying about them getting home safely."

"Yes sir. I'll do that. Thank you," I said, and hung up the telephone. I was dumbfounded. The Governor of the state of Vermont had just called me up to offer an invitation, some sound advice and a weather report. I went over to the rest of the magazine staff to tell them about this incredible thing that had just happened. They received my news and looked at me in what would have to be described as amiable toleration. They *knew* this Deane Davis I had spoken to. They weren't surprised at a gesture which, in a few short sentences, proved him to be kind, open, generous and sensible. What else did I expect? They knew the man.

But what they didn't know, back then a decade ago, was that the man was a writer. I'm not sure that he knew that either. But several years ago, he started compiling some of the stories which he'd been telling for years — the stories of his days as a country lawyer. He showed some of the stories to me and it took no particular insight on my part to know that he had a book in the making and a darned good one. "Justice in the Mountains" was published in 1980 and was an instant success.

But it came far short of exhausting Deane Davis' supply of anecdotes, tales and yarns of his days as a Vermont country lawyer and judge. I suspect this book may come short too, in exhausting the supply. But it doesn't come short in any other way. Davis writes, "I always believe stories that persist over a long period of time are either true, partly true or at least characteristic of the people and their times." The stories gathered here surely fit one of those descriptions. Mostly, I'm assured, the former.

The writer Deane Davis reminds me of two other Vermont writers, and I am reminded more of them with this book than I was with his first. I think initially of Walter Hard, Sr. when I read these marvelous tales. Hard, the author of nine volumes of poetry and a man who, at his death in 1966, was unofficially but thoroughly accepted as the poet laureate of Vermont, also wrote of the people and the rural traditions of this state he loved and honored. His ballads almost invariably were orchestrated in a steady crescendo, ending in a two line climax. Those endings are always drenched in irony and understatement—the kind that true Vermonters can dash off with complete facility and we would-be Vermonters can't even imitate. Deane Davis' stories are often built with a similar dramatic strategy. But as in Hard's unconventional verses, readers would be cheating themselves were they to skip right to the climactic punch lines. Because *getting* there is always more than half the fun. Like the skilled trial lawyer he was, Davis establishes and precisely controls the stories' tension prior to the punch. When it happens, even when we know it's coming and even when we know from what direction, it is a surprise. Invariably, a pleasant one.

The writer Deane Davis also reminds me of the writer Ralph Nading Hill—another Vermonter of multiple talents who would describe himself first as a toiler with words. The two writers have different styles but they share results. Ralph Hill once gave me the best piece of advice about writing that I will ever receive. "Writing," he said, "is hard work. Good writing is extremely hard work. And the best writing is excruciating. But when readers read the best writing, they come away thinking 'how simple that must have been to produce.'" Hill achieves that result time and again.

And so does Deane Davis. In this collection of stories, one must be impressed with the phenomenal memory which has preserved them for us. And one must be equally impressed with the variety of experience the author enjoyed and endured. But the writing itself? It seems almost effortless. One is made to believe that a marvelous story-teller and some reasonably functional recording equipment were introduced to each other and this book is the result. Those of us who have tried to achieve just that appearance of spontaneity know how erroneous that description of the process really is.

A great deal has happened in my life in the ten years since I had my first conversation with the author of this book. These days, I am so presumptuous as to call Deane Davis a friend. And when a person is asked to write an Introduction to a friend's book, a person—at least this person—is subjected to a certain apprehension. I was afraid I was going to write these words *to* Deane rather than about him. But when I finished reading this collection of stories, that fear vanished. All I was being asked to do, I realized, was introduce Deane Davis to those people who don't already know him.

Some day, no doubt, this book will be viewed as history— an account of a place and its people during some growing years. But what a marvelous history it is, what an extraordinary place it tells of, and what an extraordinary man who tells it.

Contents

Nothin' But the Truth

The Witness's Dilemma

Cross-examination is rightly called an art, for its method cannot be reduced to a set of prescribed rules. It cannot even be satisfactorily defined or described. Its principal tools are logic, drama, and psychology, but the most important of these is psychology. Its purpose is to qualify, to color, or to destroy the adverse effect of damaging testimony that the witness has already given in direct examination. Sometimes the purpose is to damage the credibility of the witness; more often the purpose is to qualify or change one statement to which the witness has already testified. Recognition of its value as an aid to the ascertainment of truth is embedded in historical experience and has resulted in the establishment of the right to confront one's accusers and to cross-examine each witness as one of the fundamentals of any judicial proceeding in all countries whose jurisprudence stems from the common law.

Cross-examination is pointless, indeed even dangerous, without a specific purpose. William Lord, a master of the art, often said that his rule was never to ask a question in cross-examination when he did not know what the answer would have to be; or unless, in cases where more than one was possible, any answer would be favorable to the examiner's side of the case. The case against Sheriff Stone illustrates how the latter procedure can work in practice.

John Stone, sheriff of Essex County, had been sued for damages by a young man whom he had arrested for robbery from the person. Stone had held the office of sheriff for thirty years, to the satisfaction of the voters of his county who re-elected him biennially with regularity, sometimes against opposition, sometimes without, but always with a substantial majority. He had enjoyed the respect of the county, and it was a crushing blow to his pride when suit was brought against him, alleging that he had practiced third-degree methods on the suspect and had used physical abuse in an attempt to secure a confession.

The newspapers of the state had given great prominence to the allegations, and several had published condemnatory editorials written from that lofty plane of editorial self-righteousness which somehow gives the impression that the allegations are true without actually so stating. There was much more at stake than the matter of money damages—this trial would decide the fate of the sheriff's job, as well as his standing in the community, which he had worked so hard to maintain and which meant so much to him.

The sheriff retained his old friend Bigelow, one of the leaders of the bar of the county, a lawyer of the old school and, incidentally, an acknowledged master of the art of cross-examination.

It was the plaintiff's claim that while the sheriff had been questioning him, the sheriff had become angry at the plaintiff's refusal to admit to any participation in the robbery and had struck the plaintiff several times on each side of the head, thrown him forcibly to the floor, and then jumped on the plaintiff's back, injuring his ribs. He also claimed that as a result of being struck on each side of the head, both eardrums had been punctured, leaving him permanently hard of hearing.

In preparing the case, Bigelow discovered that there were no other witnesses to the alleged assault. There was a witness, another jail inmate, who was prepared to testify that while the questioning had been taking place he had heard loud and angry talk on the part of the sheriff and cries of pain from Bedard, the plaintiff. Bigelow was frankly skeptical of the story of both eardrums being punctured. To him it seemed incredible that, even if force had been used, it would have resulted in the puncturing of both eardrums. Accordingly, he demanded and was granted by the court the right to have the plaintiff examined by an impartial physician. His sanguine hopes were dashed when he received Dr. Brown's report. According to the doctor, there was no question that both eardrums had been punctured. As Bigelow left the doctor's office he was quite worried and extremely puzzled. Clearly the situation looked serious for his old friend the sheriff. Yet his faith in the honor and veracity of his client was unwavering. That kind of faith in one's client is one of the attributes of a real lawyer. But Bigelow knew that it takes more than faith to win a lawsuit, and the newspaper's handling of the case, together with the natural inclination of people to believe the worst about public officials, particularly the guardians of the law, had gradually created the public belief that the plaintiff's story was true.

The day before the trial began, Bigelow sat in his office thinking about the case. Ella, his loyal and competent secretary, walked into his private room to secure his signature on some letters.

"What's the matter with you?" she asked. "You look like you've lost your last friend."

"Well, I'm going to lose my best friend or at least my best friend's case unless a miracle happens, and I don't believe in miracles."

"How's that?" asked Ella.

"The only way to break down this case is to destroy the credibility of this man Bedard. I thought we had him when he put into the complaint that story about both eardrums being broken. A good many liars are caught by the tendency to exaggerate their claims. It just doesn't seem reasonable that any man, much less Stone, would have succeeded in breaking both eardrums of a man even if he had roughed him up. But Brown says they're both broken. Looks bad to me."

"Suppose they are broken," said Ella. "That doesn't necessarily mean that Stone broke them, does it?"

Bigelow paused in the act of signing a letter, looked up at Ella with an expression that mingled surprise and hope. Dropping his pen and reaching for his hat, he said, "By golly, girl, you ought to be a lawyer. Maybe you've got something there. I'll be at Dr. Brown's."

"Doctor," said Bigelow, as he and the doctor lit a couple of Bigelow's five-cent stogies, "you say that man's eardrums are both punctured?"

"Yup, no question about it. Even a horse doctor could tell that."

"When were they broken?"

"How do I know? I wasn't there when they were broken."

"Well, I know that, but you medicos usually claim to know most everything, and I thought maybe you could tell me when they were broken."

"No, can't help you. The drums are broken, but there isn't anything about the examination to show when they were broken."

"How were they broken?"

"Can't tell you that either. They could have been broken, as Bedard claims, by a blow or they could of been broken in a dozen other ways."

"Such as how, for example?" asked Bigelow.

"Well, the most common way is by disease. Scarlet fever during childhood is the most common way I know of."

"Thanks. Have another stogie," said Bigelow as he rose and reached for his hat.

"Well, I wish I could help you," said the doctor.

"You have. See you later."

Bigelow called his secretary and informed her he was going for a ride and would be back in time for the opening of the trial in the morning.

"Where are you going?" she asked.

"Crazy, I guess," he replied, "I'm following a hunch."

Bigelow went to the garage, filled up his old battered Dodge with gas and oil, and drove to a little town in Canada where the mother of Bedard was reported to be living. After some difficulty he found her — a little elderly French lady who could not speak a word of English. He then went to the parish priest and secured his services as an interpreter. Apparently, the mother had not learned of the lawsuit, and Bigelow did not enlighten either her or the priest. The interview proceeded rather slowly and with some difficulty because of the mother's suspicion. But eventually Bigelow's hunch was corroborated. Under questioning the mother told the story of her son's serious scarlet fever illness when he was twelve years old. The infection had involved his ears to the extent that for days pus had exuded therefrom. Then Bigelow asked her if she would go to Vermont to testify. She positively and definitely refused to do so and, because the trial was to begin the following day, there was no way the testimony could be procured. Bigelow then worked far into the night dictating an affidavit covering the statements of the mother, which were laboriously written out in French and in longhand by the parish priest. The statement was signed by the mother and sworn to before the priest, and Bigelow started on his long drive back to Vermont, arriving only a few hours before the trial began.

The forenoon and early part of the afternoon were taken up with the presentation of the plaintiff's side of the case. The plaintiff was the last witness. He told his story in great detail, painting a brutal picture of the alleged assault and describing his pain and suffering in truthful fashion that made a strong impression on everyone in the courtroom, including the jury. When at last Bigelow rose to cross-examine, his instinct — highly developed during long years of courtroom experience — made him acutely aware that he faced a hostile jury. A mere denial by the sheriff would have little effect. He well knew that the only hope for his client was to utterly destroy Bedard's credibility on cross-examination.

Like the old campaigner he was, Bigelow knew exactly what he was going to try to get the witness to say, and he had given careful thought to the psychology of the situation. He had studied Bedard for hours and, with the knowledge of the family relationship obtained during the interview with the mother, had analyzed the probable reaction of the witness and mapped his course. The affidavit of the mother was not admissible as independent evidence because she was not in court; therefore the affidavit was, technically, hearsay. Bigelow had determined to make Bedard admit in cross-examination that he had had scarlet fever and that his eardrums had been seriously infected. Moreover, to emphasize and dramatize the incident, he proposed to get him first to deny it and then to force him to admit it. Bigelow had previously on cross-examination secured an admission from Dr. Sears, the plaintiff's physician, that the condition of the plaintiff's eardrums was consistent with the result of infection during scarlet fever and that punctured eardrums was a condition fairly common as a result of that disease.

"What's your age, Mr. Bedard?" asked Bigelow.

"Thirty-eight."

"Where did you live when you were twelve years old?"

"Three Rivers, Canada."

"Were you living with your mother then?"

"Yes, sir."

"Did you ever have scarlet fever?"

"Bedard hesitated a moment and then answered, "No, sir."

"Are you sure?"

"Yes, sir."

"No question about it?"

"No, sir."

"Where does your mother live now?"

"Three Rivers."

"Who is the parish priest in your mother's church?"

"Father Desilets."

"Do you know your mother's signature?"

"Yes, sir."

"Do you know Father Desilets's signature?"

"I am not sure, but I think so."

Slowly and deliberately, to heighten the effect, Bigelow extracted the original affidavit signed by Bedard's mother, and requested the court stenographer to mark it for identification. "I show you a paper marked for identification 'Defendant's 1' and call your attention to a signature near the bottom of the second page and ask you if you recognize that signature." Bigelow carefully kept the rest of the writing covered. Bedard showed considerable interest and tried desperately to read some of the rest of the writing. There was a long pause.

"Well, do you recognize it?"

"Yes," answered Bedard reluctantly.

"Whose signature is it?"

At this point Bedard's counsel, John Hay, began to evidence interest in the paper. "I object, your honor. Nothing has yet appeared showing the materiality of the paper," said Hay.

"That will appear in due course, your honor," said Bigelow.

"Objection overruled," said the judge, "he is trying to identify it."

"Whose signature is it?" repeated Bigelow.

"My mother's," said Bedard, and his expression indicated that he was suspicious of this line of questioning.

"I now call your attention to the signature on the middle of the third page. Look it over and tell us, if you can, whose signature that is."

Bedard looked the signature over long and carefully, but did not answer. After a long pause during which Bigelow's practiced eye and ear told him that the jury was getting curious, Bigelow said, "Well, do you recognize it?"

Bedard looked imploringly toward his counsel. Apparently, he got little comfort from that direction and sullenly looked at his hands and his feet.

"Come, come, Mr. Bedard, do you or don't you recognize this signature?"

"Yes," he answered in a voice barely audible.

"Whose is it?"

"Father Desilets."

"Thank you, Mr. Bedard. Now you take this paper and read it all over carefully and when you have finished I want to ask you a question."

"Your honor, I request permission to see this paper," said Mr. Hay.

"He's not entitled to see it at this point, your honor," said Bigelow. "I haven't offered it as an exhibit yet. When I get ready to offer it, if I do, I'll show it to him," said Bigelow, well knowing that he couldn't offer it because it was inadmissible.

"That's the rule, Mr. Hay," said the judge.

Hay sat down reluctantly, and it was apparent that he was puzzled and a little apprehensive. Bedard was completely immersed in reading the affidavit. Bigelow made no attempt to hurry the witness. The jury was watching the witness closely. Finally, Bedard raised his eyes and again looked imploringly at his counsel. Again he discovered no help from that quarter.

"Now," said Bigelow softly, "will you tell the jury whether you ever had scarlet fever?"

No answer. The atmosphere of the courtroom took on that certain tenseness which Bigelow had experienced many times when a high spot in the case is reached.

"Will you answer the question, Mr. Bedard?"

Still no answer. The witness clearly showed his mental distress. He could see no escape. Naturally, he shrank from admitting he had had scarlet fever so soon after having testified so positively that he had never been so afflicted. Yet if he denied it now in his own mind he would be giving the lie to his own mother and particularly to a statement of hers made before the parish priest. One alternative seemed as bad as the other. Little did he know that, if he simply denied that he had had scarlet fever, Bigelow would have been unable to contradict him.

Finally, with one last desperate look toward his own counsel, he did what Bigelow knew he would do—what witnesses usually will do when confronted with so hopeless a dilemma—he told the truth.

"Did you have scarlet fever, Mr. Bedard?"

"Yes," he answered in a voice so low it could scarcely be heard.

"Did it infect your ears?"

"Yes."

"Did pus run from your ears?"

"Yes."

As the jury settled back into their chairs, Bigelow knew when to stop.

"That's all," he said.

The verdict was for the sheriff.

The Sheriff Doubts

In Vermont, tradition has for many years required a proclamation at the opening of each term of county court and likewise in the Supreme Court. This tradition is deeply embedded in the long history of the development of the common law of England and the judicial system of this country. The proclamation is given orally by the court officer, who is usually the sheriff of the county or one of the deputies, when called upon by the presiding judge.

In the first term of Lamoille County Court at which I presided, our court officer was the new sheriff of Lamoille County, just elected. He was a good officer and a good sheriff, and he took his duties very seriously. Knowing that he would be required to make a proclamation at the opening of the next term in his county, he had attended the opening of a term of court in the Supreme Court to observe the manner in which the court officer handled the matter in that august tribunal.

I was a young judge. Appointed at the age of thirty, I was at that time the second youngest superior-court judge ever to have been appointed. The Honorable Harry B. Chase, who later became a Supreme Court justice and then a judge of the 2d Circuit Court of Appeals, was the youngest. I'm sure that I looked quite young to the old-timers around the courthouse as well as to the new sheriff. I felt young and inexperienced, and doubtless that showed to some degree upon my countenance. So perhaps you can imagine how I felt when, at my direction, the sheriff proceeded to deliver the proclamation. He read from a piece of paper lying on the sheriff's podium as follows:

> Hear ye, hear ye, hear ye. The Honorable County Court and the Court of Chancery in and for the County of Lamoille is now open for business. All ye that have business before this Honorable Court draw nigh that ye may be heard.

And then, pausing for what seemed to me altogether too long and looking at me with a speculative glance, he closed his formal proclamation with these words:

> "God save the state of Vermont."

An Obliging Lawyer

Country lawyers often find themselves in positions where their services are required under most informal and unusual circumstances.

Late in the afternoon, while mowing my lawn, I suddenly experienced intense pain in my lower abdomen. I ceased my lawn mowing and went inside to rest. No relief. Gradually, I found myself doubled over, with the pain just as severe. So I called Dr. John Woodruff and explained my symptoms. "Well," he said, "sounds like appendicitis, but get over here right away and I'll examine you." My wife was away for a few days so I was alone in the house and drove myself to the doctor's office. He examined me and confirmed to his original diagnosis. Under his instructions I drove myself to the hospital, and some time later he arrived at the hospital and examined me again and ordered a blood test taken. A couple of hours later the doctor came to see me in my hospital room and informed me that because of the results of the blood test he was going to operate that night.

It was about 9:30 when they came to take me to the operating room. By the time I arrived there, I was quite sleepy from a shot that had been administered in my room. I was, however, awake enough to greet the nurses, whom I knew, Dr. Avery, the anesthetist, and Dr. Woodruff, the surgeon. Dr. Avery clamped a mask over my face, and as I inhaled ether I found myself getting fuzzy almost at once. While still a bit aware of my surroundings, I saw Dr. E. H. Bailey, a long-time client of mine, enter the room with a flourish. "Where's Deane Davis?" he asked. He was informed that I was on the operating table, under anesthetic, and about to be operated on. "Well bring him out, I've got an emergency job for him." I was barely conscious of a bit of argument between the doctors, but ultimately Dr. Bailey prevailed, the mask was removed, and gradually the world came back into focus. Dr. Bailey then informed me that he had a patient on the second floor of the hospital who would not live until morning and that she wanted to make a will. Dr. Bailey had informed himself as to his patient's intentions and how she wanted her property disposed of. He assured me that his patient was fully conscious and possessed testamentary capacity.

I asked him to summon one of the secretaries from the administrative office of the hospital, but none being available because it was so long after office hours, we pressed one of the nurses into service. I dictated the will to the nurse, who wrote it down in long hand. I then directed Dr. Bailey as to the formalities of execution.

I woke up in the middle of the night, after dreaming for what seemed hours about flying above the clouds. The light was on. Two men with an undertaker's basket came into my distorted view. I was sure they were after me. Then I recognized the two men. One was the funeral director from Chelsea, and the other was his assistant. I heard the director say "Hell, Henry, we must be in the wrong room. This man ain't dead." I hoped he was right.

In the morning Dr. Bailey dropped in to see me and reported that his patient had died during the night. She had executed her will, and her wishes would be carried out.

A country lawyer's life may not always be happy. But at least he'll never be bored.

An Eye for the Truth

Judge Allen Sturtevant of Middlebury, Vermont, was a good lawyer, later served as a superior-court judge, and still later was elevated to the Supreme Court of Vermont. In all of these capacities he was a great success. He was a careful and close student of the law, he possessed a quick and alert intelligence, and he was an excellent judge of human nature and motivations. Sturtevant was also something of a wag. He was quick to recognize and appreciate humorous situations and equally quick and adept at creating humor. His eyes were very bad, however. Even his ordinary glasses were many times thicker than usual. When required to read, he had to wear special glasses with lenses unlike anything I had ever seen. On one eye the lenses were so constructed that they bore a resemblance to a telescope. On this eye the lenses protruded a couple of inches in front of the pupil. He often wore these special lenses while presiding in court when there were large numbers of papers involved in the case, either as pleadings or as exhibits.

On one occasion, when I had a case for trial in Bennington County Court, Judge Sturtevant was presiding. I had

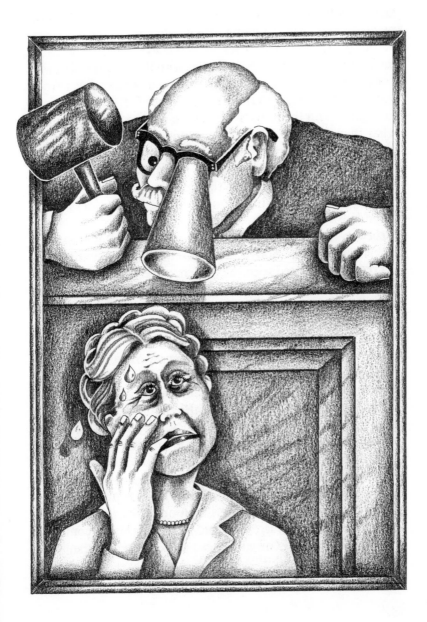

arrived in Bennington the day before because I did not know precisely when the preceding case would end. In the morning, before court convened, a few of the lawyers had gathered in the judge's chamber to swap stories with the judge, which was not uncommon in his court. Among them was a lawyer from out of state who had not previously met the judge. He was fascinated with the judge's special glasses and asked the judge what they were for. The judge jokingly replied, "Well these glasses enable me to look right into a witness's mind and tell me whether he is telling the truth or not."

Shortly the bell rang, and the case ahead of me proceeded. There was only one witness, an elderly lady. Counsel for the defendant, who had offered the witness, seemed much perturbed at the testimony of his own witness. But Stafford, father of Senator Stafford, counsel for the plaintiff, appeared quite pleased with the evidence and waived any cross-examination. The case thereupon ended, and because it was tried without a jury, the judge reserved decision and ordered a recess of one-half hour, following which my case would be heard.

The lawyers gathered in the lawyers' room during this recess. After a lapse of fifteen minutes or so, Stafford came into the room chuckling. He had done a little investigation on his own as to why the witness testified quite differently than he expected and quite satisfactorily for the plaintiff's case. So we asked him the reason for his amusement.

Still chuckling he said, "Well you know I had taken the deposition of that witness some months ago, and her testimony was adverse to the plaintiff. But she was standing in the hall this morning just outside the door of the judge's chambers when Judge Sturtevant said that his glasses could see right into the minds of witnesses and tell whether they were telling the truth or not."

Not a Crystal

Justice Oliver Wendell Holmes, in one of his scholarly opinions, once wrote, "A word is not a crystal, unchanging for all time. It is but the skin of a living thought, which varies greatly according to the time and circumstances in which used."

Harley Buchanan ran a small trucking business in Barre during the early days of trucks in Vermont. He employed a helper who was always behind in his bills and hence had accumulated a reputation for being something of a deadbeat. The helper, Charlie Curtis, went into McWhorter's clothing store on Main Street in Barre to buy a suit of clothes. After he had picked out a suit that pleased him, he told the clerk he would take it. Then he told the clerk he would like to be trusted for it. The clerk called the manager, and following a preliminary discussion between the three of them, the manager said that he would trust him if he could find somebody to "go good for you." Charlie said that his boss Buchanan would go good for him and suggested that the manager call Buchanan and get his guarantee. The manager called Buchanan and the conversation, according to the records, went as follows:

"Mr. Buchanan, this is McWhorter's store."

"Yes."

"Charlie Curtis is here and wants to buy a suit of clothes and I have told him I will trust him if he gets somebody to go good for him. He tells me that you will."

"How much is the suit?"

"Seventy-five dollars."

"Well, *if Charlie refuses to pay I will.*"

The manager thereupon told Buchanan, "O.K. You write me a letter and I'll let Charlie have the suit." The letter was promptly sent, but Buchanan was careful to use in the letter precisely the same words he had used in his telephone conversation, that is: "If Charlie refuses to pay I will."

Charlie didn't pay. Neither did he specifically *refuse* to pay. In due course McWhorter's demanded payment from Buchanan. Buchanan refused to pay. He said that he had never guaranteed the account, that he knew Charlie would never pay, and that he used the language he did expecting McWhorter's to understand that he was in effect refusing to guarantee the account and that McWhorter's should have understood that and refused to let Charlie have the suit. "I told you that if Charlie refused to pay I would, which of course means that if Charlie refused to pay *I would refuse.*"

The case soon became a cause célèbre in Barre after McWhorter's brought suit in Barre City Court against Buchanan. Buchanan still refused to pay.

The case dragged on for some time—during which it became the talk of the town—and then it came on for trial by jury. There was much hilarity in the court room, but McWhorter's and Buchanan were in dead earnest. The jury took more than five hours in its deliberations. Acting with sound common sense, the jury apparently adopted Justice Holmes's philosophy; they treated the words as "not crystal clear," interpreting them "according to the time and circumstances in which used," and held Buchanan liable as guarantor for the seventy-five dollars.

Boomerang

Hardly anyone today hears about the pound keeper. Or even knows what one is. But he used to be an important town officer in the days when almost everybody in Vermont kept animals of some kind. Fences covered long distances and were prone to disrepair. Animals have a penchant for discovering holes or weak spots in fences, so they often strayed, looking for greener pastures, and sometimes strayed so far that no one in the vicinity could identify either the animal or its owners. Thus the need in each town for a pound keeper. Stray animals that could not be identified were taken to him for care and safekeeping. Under the law the pound keeper was then required to advertise the animal for three weeks in "a newspaper circulating in the county." He was required to describe the animal and to give notice that unless the animal was claimed and all charges paid within the three-week period, the animal would be sold at public auction on a date specified in the notice.

Vermonters, being thrifty individuals, had provided no reimbursement for the pound keeper out of town funds. Instead they had provided in the statute that that officer should be reimbursed by the owner if the animal was retrieved prior to the sale, and if not, should be reimbursed out of the proceeds of the sale. The statute was a bit nebulous in providing what were the legal charges due the pound keeper: it provided that he should be entitled to receive "all reasonable charges."

Don Camp, who owned and operated a farm in South Barre, was the pound keeper for Barre Town. One day a Barre Town resident came to the pound leading a fine up-headed, well-balanced three-year-old chestnut colt. He explained that he had found the colt wandering on East Hill, that he had caught the colt and placed him in his barn for a few days expecting to find the owner. When inquiry failed to discover the owner he had decided to bring him to the pound. Don was a client of mine, so he came to me for advice and help in following the technical directions of the statute and in preparing the necessary notices and documents. I told Don that because, apparently, no one was going to claim the horse he had better tack on everything he could think of that could even imaginably be included under the phrase "all reasonable charges." Working together, we did a pretty good job in that direction. We ran up a bill of $128.75.

On the day of the auction sale, pursuant to Don's request, I drove out to Don's farm. Don had said that he would feel more comfortable if I was there in case any questions should arise.

As I got out of my car and walked up the driveway toward his barn, I saw that a large crowd of people were on hand, either to bid on the horse or to see the fun. Slowly working my way through the crowd, shaking hands with people I knew, I was nearly at the barn doorway before I saw the horse cross-tied on the barn floor.

I was shocked. It was my horse.

When the crowd caught on to the fact, there was loud clapping of hands and boisterous laughter—and much red faced embarrassment on my part. It cost me $128.75 to redeem my own colt. I rued the day when I taught Don how to run up the bill!

Exhibit A

Mrs. Webster, widow, lived in Waits River village in a home beside the main road, which leads through the village. Living in the home with her was Tom Conlin, who operated a filling station directly across the road. Gossip had it that the filling station had been built and equipped by Mrs. Webster. It was also noticed by the neighbors that Mrs. Webster had purchased a new car and Conlin chauffered her wherever she wanted to go, including a trip to Florida. Conlin, before coming to Waits River, had owned and operated a large milk-distributing business in Newburyport, Massachusetts. Married, he had experienced marital troubles and had been separated from his wife for quite some time before coming to Vermont.

Mrs. Webster came to my office one day and presented me with a writ, complaint, and summons in which she was named defendant. The action was brought by the wife of Mr. Conlin and was returnable before the Orange County Court. Mrs. Webster asked me to represent her in the action.

The complaint charged that Mrs. Webster had maliciously alienated the affections of the plaintiff's husband, which caused her much mental distress and suffering for all of which she asked the court to grant her the sum of $50,000 in actual and exemplary damages. In those days suits for alienation of affection were fairly common. They are practically a thing of the past now, another indication of the changing of social values that has occurred over the last fifty years.

The case came on for trial by jury at Chelsea, the county seat, during the month of December. Suffice it to say that the evidence, though sharply contradicted, did show the high probability of more than a brotherly and sisterly relationship between Mrs. Webster and her boarder. But there was also some testimony concerning a Mr. Johnson in Newburyport who, it appeared, had been squiring the plaintiff. And Conlin testified that the relationship between Johnson and Mrs. Conlin was quite unplatonic. In other words, one of the claims in our defense was that even if Mrs. Webster had to some extent alienated the affections of Conlin from his wife, nevertheless the conduct of Mrs. Conlin and Johnson showed that the Conlin marriage had deteriorated before Conlin came to Waits River and met Mrs. Webster. If, therefore, Conlin had no substantial affection for his wife at the time Conlin and Mrs. Webster first met, Mrs. Conlin had no substantial basis upon which to base her claim.

The difficulty was that, because of the expense involved, we did not have any witnesses from Newburyport on this aspect of the case except Conlin himself, whose word was unsupported. Fortunately, however, Mr. Johnson gallantly accompanied Mrs. Conlin to Vermont and lent his comfort and support during the hectic several days of the trial. Because Chelsea is a small compact village, and because there was only one hotel in Chelsea where judges, lawyers, jurors, and witnesses all ate their meals, the constant companionship between Mrs. Conlin and Johnson did not go unnoticed and did attract enough attention so that there was considerable speculation as to who this handsome gentleman in the coonskin coat might be and exactly what his relationship to Mrs. Conlin was. Although Johnson's name had been mentioned frequently in both Conlin's and Mrs. Conlin's testimony, there still wasn't much helpful testimony on the record, other than Conlin's statement, to support the idea of the unplatonic relationship between Mrs. Conlin and Johnson. But it was quite apparent as the trial wore on, from the attitude toward each other there in Chelsea, that Johnson and Mrs. Conlin had something going. But I felt it would still be necessary to dramatize this for the jury. How? On the final day of the presentation of the defense witnesses, the solution occurred to me. Johnson each day had sat in the last row of seats in the courtroom, obviously trying to be as inconspicuous as possible. So, at the very end of our case, I asked if Mr. Charles Johnson was in the room. Of course, I knew he was. After some hesitation Mr. Johnson identified himself. I asked him to take the witness chair, which he did. The examination went like this.

"Will you please state your name for the record?"

"Mr. Charles Johnson."

"Where do you live, Mr. Johnson?"

"242 Lincoln Street, Newburyport, Massachusetts."

"Thank you, Mr. Johnson, that is all."

Consternation broke out in the courtroom. Counsel for the plaintiff in an angry voice accused me of unethical conduct and moved that the court reprimand me for such conduct and direct the jury to draw no inferences from Johnson's appearance on the stand. Thereupon the court excused the jury from the courtroom so that the situation could be argued before the court without prejudicing the jury.

The presiding judge then addressed me and said, "Mr. Davis, I have never known of a situation like this happening in court. I would like to know if you have."

"No, your honor."

"You knew, Mr. Davis, when you called Johnson to the stand that you were not going to ask him any question other than his name and address, did you not?"

"Yes, your honor."

"And to prejudice the jury against the plaintiff?"

"No, your honor. The purpose, your honor, was to offer Mr. Johnson as an exhibit in the case so that the jury could see for themselves just who this individual was who had been referred to in the testimony already on the record from the plaintiff and Tom Conlin."

The argument of counsel on both sides then waxed long and loud as to the propriety of such conduct. The presiding judge was becoming more perplexed as the argument wore on.

Thereupon the presiding judge announced a recess, and the three judges repaired to chambers. They were there for almost an hour. Finally the bell rang, and the judges ascended the bench. The court reporter assumed her place at the reporter's desk. And the judge directed the following entry: "The Court rules that there was no impropriety in presenting Mr. Johnson as an exhibit in this case."

It worked. The jury returned a verdict for the defendant.

A Lack of Confidence

In the early twenties in Vermont we were still in the transition stage between horses and automobiles as a means of transportation. This circumstance affected the attitude of people toward what was due care and what was negligence in the handling of automobiles. The prosecution that follows would never happen today, now that practically everybody drives a car.

Dean Rollins, a valued employee of the Granite City Cooperative Creamery in Barre, was driving his company's truck in the town of Tunbridge. As he left the village of Tunbridge going north, he came to a covered bridge that was just about wide enough for two cars to pass. The highway on both ends of the bridge curved a bit as it approached the bridge, which obscured the view from drivers coming both north and south to enter the bridge. Rollins was traveling on the right side of the highway as he approached the entrance on his end of the bridge. Jones was driving his Dodge car into the bridge from the other end going south. The only other passenger in Jones's car was his four-year-old grandson, who was standing up on the passenger's side of the front seat leaning against the back of the seat. As he entered the bridge, Jones was on the left side of the highway, the wrong side from the direction in which he was traveling. Rollins observed the Jones car on the wrong side of the road. Because he saw no sign of the Jones car pulling to its right, Rollins pulled his truck to his left and the wrong side of the road. Just as Rollins headed for his left, Jones headed for his right. The result was inevitable. A bad collision. And sadly, the force of the impact threw the four-year-old into the windshield. The windshield shattered, and the grandson was severely cut about the neck; an artery was severed, and in spite of first aid rendered at the scene, the child died.

Shortly thereafter, the state's attorney for Orange County prosecuted Rollins for manslaughter because of the death of Jones's grandson on the theory that he, Rollins, was on the wrong side of the road at the moment of impact.

At the close of the evidence, I debated filing a motion for a directed verdict on the ground that, taking the evidence in the light most favorable to the prosecution, there was no evidence of negligence justifying submission of the case to the jury. But I finally concluded that there was *some* evidence, and if so a directed verdict would not be granted at that stage of the case.

The case was fully argued on both sides, the jury was instructed by the judge on the law applicable, and the jury retired to consider the verdict. All afternoon and evening and during the forenoon of the next day the jury wrestled with the case. After the noon recess of the second day of their deliberations, the jury came into court and reported that they were in hopeless disagreement. They were excused. We later learned that the jury stood six for guilty and six for not guilty throughout the whole of their deliberations.

The jury was excused. Fortunately, the case was never tried again.

About a month after the trial I met Judge Thompson, who had presided. He said to me, "Why didn't you file a motion for a directed verdict in favor of your client in that Rollins case in Chelsea?"

"Why, Judge, I did consider it but came to the conclusion you would have to deny it as a matter of law."

"Well, if you had filed the motion I would have granted it."

This taught me a lesson that I never forgot. I never tried a case, civil or criminal, after that in which I did not move for a directed verdict—no matter whether I thought the motion was valid or not.

After a "hung jury" it is customary for the prosecuting officer to review the case in the light of all the evidence produced at the trial and in the light of the jury's disagreement, and make a judgment as to whether the case should be retried. The prosecutor did so and concluded the chances were slim for a conviction and hence exercised his discretion to drop the case.

Bewitched

The strident ringing of the telephone awakened me from my usual Sunday afternoon nap. It was John Peterson, son-in-law of a Barre Town resident named McKinstry. Peterson informed me that he was calling from the Washington County Jail, where his father-in-law was being detained for questioning on a charge of murder. He said that his father-in-law wanted a lawyer. I soon found out he surely needed one. I told Peterson to tell his father-in-law to talk to no one until I arrived there. Inside of twenty minutes I arrived and was greeted by Henry Lawson, county sheriff, and informed that McKinstry had failed to heed my instructions about keeping his mouth shut and in that twenty minutes had signed a written confession to the charge. From Lawson and later from my client I gathered the basic facts.

McKinstry was a sixty-year-old widower with four daughters. Two of them were married, and two were living at home with McKinstry. For some time he had employed as a housekeeper a Mrs. Russell, a married woman twenty-six years old. Mrs. Russell's husband was at that time serving a sentence in the state prison at Windsor. As time went on, Mrs. Russell voluntarily enlarged her housekeeping responsibilities by warming her employer's bed. Everything went smoothly until after a year or so Russell was paroled from state's prison, came home to Roxbury, rented an old farmhouse, retrieved his wife, and set up housekeeping in the new Roxbury home.

McKinstry became very unhappy at this separation. He brooded over his unhappy fate and made a number of surreptitious trips to the Roxbury home, endeavoring to entice his former housekeeper back to his bed and board. All to no avail. Finally, he came to the conclusion that if he could get rid of Russell in some way he would be able to achieve his goal.

As my investigation proceeded, other pertinent and disheartening facts emerged. McKinstry had purchased a box of shells to fit his shotgun and had begun practicing at a mark set up in his back yard. This practice continued for a couple of weeks prior to the shooting. Then on the fatal day, after his day's work in the granite shed, McKinstry bought a pint of whiskey and took it home with him. He imbibed a couple of strong drinks to fortify his courage and went out to the back yard and took a couple of shots at the mark to assure himself that he was in good form and drove to Roxbury. There he parked his car out of sight off the main road and crawled up a long, steep bank to the Russell home. By this time it was quite dark. The living room of the farmhouse was well lighted with kerosene lamps. Taking careful aim at Russell, who was seated in a chair near the window, he pulled the trigger, turned, and ran down the bank to his car. In his excitement he drove too fast, or perhaps the liquor was having an effect. In any event, after driving only a couple of miles toward Montpelier he managed to get his right front wheel off the blacktop into some loose sand, which, because of his excessive speed, pulled the right end of the car too far off the road; the car struck a guardrail, which in turn propelled the car into a complete

180-degree turn, and the car wound up facing back toward Roxbury. The car was wedged against the guardrail and so far embedded in loose sand that it couldn't move. McKinstry was much agitated by the situation in which he now found himself. His first thought was to divest himself of the murder weapon. He threw it over a steep bank beside his car, where it was later found. The bank was fully covered by heavy brush and concealed the weapon completely. McKinstry wondered how he was going to extricate himself. Before he reached a solution a car appeared driving toward Roxbury from Montpelier. It proved to be Henry Lawson, the sheriff, who had been alerted by telephone to the shooting and was on his way to investigate. Lawson stopped to see what the motorist's trouble was. Because the car was facing toward the Russell home instead of away from it, it did not occur to Lawson that the motorist could be in any way connected with the shooting. Lawson quickly helped McKinstry get his car back on the road and proceeded on his way to the Russell home to perform his official duty.

In a few days Lawson's investigation inevitably began to point the finger of suspicion toward McKinstry. McKinstry was brought in to the county jail for questioning, and he ultimately signed the written confession to the shooting and the circumstances surrounding it. Thereupon he was remanded to jail to await the action of the grand jury. A special grand jury was called and promptly indicted McKinstry for first-degree murder. At that time the statutes of Vermont provided for mandatory execution for first-degree murder.

At that point Albert A. Sargent of Barre joined me as associate counsel for the defense. Sargent was an able lawyer and a well-known champion of lost causes.

Sargent and I had many conferences in an attempt to find a credible basis for a defense. As the date of trial drew near, we were struggling to find anything that could be said in defense. On the facts it would appear to be the worst case of premeditated murder one could imagine. The strong motive of McKinstry to recover his housekeeper and bed companion, his persistent efforts to persuade Mrs. Russell to return, setting up the mark in the back yard followed by two weeks of practice shooting, the liquor and the final practice shots on the fatal day, the long drive to Roxbury, the crawl up the bank in the dark, and shooting from the dark into a lighted room were fairly indicative of premeditation. And premeditation constituted first-degree murder. And first-degree murder would result automatically in execution.

We had, of course, told the accused and his family that conviction for murder was inevitable in view of the confession; that the only possible question was whether premeditation could be established; and that anything other than conviction of first-degree murder was only a slim hope.

The night before the trial began I couldn't sleep. The frustration of this case kept me tossing and turning. Eventually, I got up and put on my bathrobe and went downstairs. But this was no relief. I paced the living room as my mind churned in frantic attempts to find just one little thing that could be said for the accused on the question of premeditation. One could say that this was senseless reaction on my part. Possibly. But trial lawyers, if they are worth their salt, "marry" their cases and identify completely with the interest of the client. This is particularly so in criminal cases.

As I paced the living room in search for a ray of light, the upstairs bedroom door opened and my wife, dressed in her bathrobe, came downstairs to join me.

"What's the matter, honey?" she said.

"It's this damn murder case."

"Well, what about it?" she asked.

"I just haven't got one single defense."

"Well, sit down and tell me about it."

So we sat on the couch and I told her the whole story. When I had finished she said, "I think you've got a clear defense!"

"What, for heaven's sake?"

"Why, the man was bewitched." As she talked on about the accused, a man of sixty years of age, and his relationship with a girl of twenty-six and what can happen to the male mind under such circumstances, suddenly I did see a ray of light. I recalled an article by Justice Cardozo, then of the U.S. Supreme Court, in which, in his usual masterful fashion, he had analyzed the crime of murder and the constituent elements of its several degrees. Cardozo's article makes it abundantly clear, contrary to the general impression, that the line of demarcation between first- and second-degree murder is quite fuzzy indeed. For example, in spite of the centuries during which the common law has evolved and the volumes of decisions of courts of last resort, there is still not a completely satisfactory way to define the difference between intent and premeditation. The result is that the resolution of that question, in the last analysis, becomes the duty of the jury, with far less actual guidance by the court and far more latitude than is the case in most situations with which juries have to contend. Anyway, the suggestion by my wife that the accused was bewitched, taken in conjunction with my memory of the Cardozo article, gave me the cue I was looking for.

All because my wife, bless her, unencumbered by a knowledge and preoccupation with the technicalities of the law, could see clearly what really caused this killing. The accused *was* bewitched. No killing would have occurred except for that fact. And it involved the mental state of the accused. Not that he was insane. But because he was bewitched we would claim that he was incapable of that extra degree of "pondering the consequences" of his act that constitutes premeditation under the law.

Not a bright prospect, surely, but at least something to talk about in defense.

I went back to bed and slept soundly.

Early the next morning, before court convened, Sargent and I met by prearrangement. We discussed this proposed strategy. He accepted it wholeheartedly. I felt sure that he would because there was no other alternative.

The prosecuting attorneys were Cornelius Granai, Esq., then state's attorney of the county, and J. Ward Carver, Esq., then attorney general of the state, who under the law as it was then was required to personally assist in the prosecution of murder cases. Both these men were experienced and skillful trial lawyers.

The opening statement on the part of the prosecution was a full portrayal of all the facts described above and an assurance to the jury that the evidence of the prosecution would establish that. And he stated that the state would ask for a verdict of first-degree murder.

Our statement was very brief — merely that we agreed with most of the facts described in the prosecution's opening statement but that we would present clear and convincing evidence that the accused was incapable of "premeditation" and that therefore he should not be convicted of first-degree murder. I'm sure that the presiding judge was puzzled by this statement, because of both its brevity and its novelty. He called counsel to the bench and asked us if we claimed the accused was insane. We said "no." His countenance continued to show his puzzlement. Then he said, "What is the defense in this case?" I answered, "The accused was bewitched." "Bewitched?" he said, "is that a defense of murder?" "We think so, your

Honor." "How?" asked the judge. "That will be developed as the case progresses," I said, hoping the judge would not force me to expand further at that time. He didn't. He was an old-time criminal lawyer himself. There was a twinkle in his eye as he put his hand up to his mouth to conceal the smile that I was sure was there.

The presentation of the state's evidence took about two days. We did not put the accused on the stand. We thought that the sordid story was told in the written confession as favorably for the accused as it ever could be. And we did not want to submit him to cross-examination by either one of these skillful prosecutors.

Our "clear and convincing evidence" that the accused was incapable of premeditation consisted almost entirely of testimony of the four daughters of the accused. They were stellar witnesses, mild in manner, polite and ladylike throughout. And it was convincing of one thing at least—that the accused was completely overboard in his infatuation for his housekeeper, even to the degree that his infatuation was the one controlling influence in his life for months before the fatal day. Nor were they crossed up in any way by vigorous cross-examination. But, of course, the real test was yet to come. We knew it would come and hoped it might be delayed until our argument before the jury since it would be more dramatic then and closer to the point of final decision by the jury. We knew the prosecuting attorneys would at some point contest the theory on which our whole case depended and would most likely raise the question when we started to argue the point that the infatuation of the accused resulted in his being bewitched to the point that he was unable mentally to be guilty of premeditation. We expected opposing counsel to take the position that bewitchment was not as a matter of law excuse for conduct that otherwise would clearly amount to premeditation.

40

Following the testimony of the oldest daughter, a recess was declared. During the recess the court officer came into the lawyer's room and announced that the judge wanted to see counsel in chambers immediately. We found the three judges all wearing solemn countenances, and the court reporter was in place at her table. The judge then announced that the court officer had reported to him during recess that when the jury filed out of the courtroom down the hall to the jury room the door to the courtroom opened. As it did, the eldest daughter of the accused started to come out into the hall, then seeing the jury filing by she stepped back into the doorway to let them pass. As the jury filed by the spot where she was standing, one of the jurors stuck out his hand and shook hands with her. The judge further said that he felt that this impropriety would have to be examined and the evidence placed on the record. So, in turn, the officer and the juror were each called to testify concerning the incident. The judge did most of the interrogation.

The juror admitted that the incident took place, said he did not know that it was an impropriety, and insisted that it was not an indication of any prejudice on his part; he said that he had not yet made up his mind about the case and that the incident would not affect his judgment in any way. Then the judge sent for the daughter. How I wished that I might have a few minutes with her before she testified. But of course that was impossible under the circumstances. To my surprise, she again made an excellent witness. Asked if the incident took place she answered: "Why yes. Did I do something wrong?"

Truth is a powerful weapon, and candor has its own ability to transform a suspicious incident into a completely innocent act. You could feel the tension evaporate in the room. Whereupon the attorney general addressed the court and said,

"I don't think there was anything wrong in this incident. The state is satisfied and will not move for a mistrial. We're willing to proceed."

I heaved a sigh of relief.

But my troubles were not over. Just as the recess was nearing its end and I was to go into court for the argument for the defense, the court officer came to me and said that the accused insisted on seeing me before we went back into court. I stepped to the judge's chambers and asked for a ten-minute extension of recess, which was promptly granted. Then I went to the witness room, where the accused was kept during the various recesses of the court, and talked with him alone. He was quite agitated. I asked him what he wanted.

"There's something I gotta tell you."

"Does it relate to the case?" I asked.

"Yes, it does," he said, "but I want you to agree not to bring it out in court."

"Is it important?" I asked.

"Yes, it is."

"Well, this is one hell of a time to be telling me about it. But let's have it."

"Well, you see, Mrs. Russell and I had agreed that I would shoot her husband and had agreed on the date. And she told me that she would get him in a chair by the window after supper."

My response to this shocking statement is unprintable.

In a few minutes the bell rang signaling the end of recess, and I went into court to make the argument on behalf of the accused. Almost immediately after I commenced the argument directed toward the issue of bewitchment and premeditation, the attorney general arose and addressed the court:

"Your Honor, we object to this line of argument. There is no claim of insanity or evidence of insanity in the case. The evidence of premeditation is overwhelming. We ask the court to rule on the issue and thus avoid constant interruption of the counsel's argument."

The presiding judge, knowing that this was our whole defense in the case, wisely excused the jury while we could argue the law in the case, prior to his ruling. As soon as the jury had retired, the presiding judge said: "Do you have any authority for the proposition that infatuation, or bewitchment as you call it, is pertinent to the question of premeditation?"

"No, your Honor, except the authority of simple logic."

"Well, in that case, I think you had better develop your theory of logic in question."

Using the Cardozo article as the basis of my argument, I proceeded to establish the point that the line of demarcation between "intent" and "premeditation" was indeed far from clear. And I wound up my argument with the following words: "The question here is the state of mind of the accused. The jury in order to find a verdict of first-degree murder must find that premeditation did actually exist at or about the time of the fatal shooting. It is not enough to prove that it existed at some time previous to the shooting. It is not a question of whether infatuation can be a defense for murder. The question is to what extent did his infatuation, his bewitchment, affect the mind of the accused. Did it so affect his mind that in fact he did not actually premeditate? In the absence of insanity the existence of intent to kill is presumed by the nature of the act. But premeditation is a quality of mind that goes beyond the normal mental process of forming an intent. It is an affirmative mental act. A process of weighing, considering, recalling the nature and quality of the act and thus after such consideration a decision to go ahead and commit the unlawful act. I realize premeditation requires no particular interval of time. It can occur in seconds. *But it must occur.* And the jury must find that it did in fact occur. And no one else but the jury can make that decision. A ruling by the court that premeditation did not occur would be reversible error. The court can and must charge the jury as to what is premeditation but to say that it did not occur under these circumstances would be an improper invasion of the province of the jury."

The three judges thereupon retired to the seclusion of the judge's chambers to consider their ruling. They were gone for what seemed an eternity, but it was in fact about a half-hour. Then the court sent for the officer to bring the jury back into court. The judges mounted the bench, and the court ruled as follows:

"The court holds that there is a substantial difference between intent and premeditation. At the conclusion of the arguments of counsel, we will define for the jury the nature and meaning of both intent and premeditation. We hold that the affirmative finding of premeditation is the province of the jury and that counsel for the defense has a right to argue to the jury the theory that has been presented, and of course counsel for the state has a right to argue the contrary. You may proceed, Mr. Davis."

Following the conclusion of the argument of counsel, the presiding judge delivered an excellent charge to the jury in which he summarized the legal authorities on the question of intent and premeditation.

The jury retired to consider its verdict. After several hours of anxious waiting, the jury announced it was ready to report and filed into court for that purpose.

Verdict: guilty of murder in the *second* degree.

He was *"bewitched."*

On Counting Sheep

In the early 1930s, while serving as a superior judge, I was holding court in St. Albans, the county seat of Franklin County.

Whenever there was a lull in the business of the court, I enjoyed chatting with George Stevens, the county clerk. He was a gruff, irascible character with a lot of this world's experience behind him and a country philosopher of the first order.

One day I walked into his office and found him in a foul mood indeed. This was in the early days of the New Deal, when the administration in Washington was trying to counter the Great Depression with a long list of make-work projects. Among them was one by the U.S. Department of Agriculture to construct an inventory of all farm animals in the United States. An ambitious project, to say the least.

Sensing Stevens's mood, I asked him what was bothering him. "I'll tell you what's bothering me. Here, look at this," he said, handing me a letter from the Department of Agriculture asking him immediately to report to the department the number of sheep in Franklin County.

"And here, you might as well see my reply." He handed

me the copy he had personally pounded out on his ancient Ollivet typewriter. It went like this:

There is no record in this office of the number of sheep in Franklin County. I know of no place in the state where there is a record of the number of sheep in Franklin County. The only way to find out how many sheep there are in Franklin County is to go out and and count them. And I'm too damn busy.

Harmony by Law

One of the duties that used to occupy much of the time of superior judges was to hear petitions to enforce court orders previously issued in divorce cases. Those were the days before we were blessed with career women. Usually, there was only one wage earner, and that was the husband. Hence, in most cases, an important part of the process of hearing and disposing of a divorce case was to adjudicate a proper amount of money to be paid the wife for the support of herself and minor children. Also, of course, if there was property it was necessary to make appropriate orders for its division. The law gave few directions as to what the guiding rules were in the case of the disposition of real or personal property. Perhaps this was just as well, for cases differed so much on their facts that to write specific rules would be a practical impossibility. So the law fell back on its old cliché, "reasonable," probably the most overworked word in judicial lexicon.

Often these orders for support were not complied with—sometimes because of inability and sometimes out of sheer malice. More often than not it was because of changed circumstances. Orders that were quite reasonable at the time of granting the divorce soon became unreasonable because of changed circumstances. Remarriage of one or both of the parties was a frequent cause. The remedy for the wife to enforce compliance was to petition the court asking that the recalcitrant husband be held in contempt of court for his failure to comply with the order. If the court adjudged the husband to be in contempt, he could be committed to jail unless he complied. Contempt proceedings thus became a powerful weapon for enforcement.

I heard many of these cases. One in particular stands out in my memory. It was a petition addressed to me as a superior judge and heard at the Orange County Courthouse, in Chelsea. In this case the parties had been divorced three years previously by order of the county court. An order had been made by the court in which all of the property comprising a hill farm in Vershire and the cattle and farm machinery had been decreed to the wife. In addition, the court ordered the husband to pay his former wife four dollars a week toward the support of two minor children of the parties. The husband had paid the four dollars a week regularly for about a year and then stopped. He had made no payments since. He testified that the reason he stopped was because about that time his former wife had remarried and so had he. To complicate the case further, the husband and his new wife had become parents of a baby girl. The ex-husband testified that the only work he could get was as a hired man on a farm; that the highest wage he had been able to earn since the divorce was forty dollars a month and "found," as it used to be called. "Found" meant that his compensation, in addition to the forty dollars a week, was to include living quarters, wood for fuel, and eggs, milk, and vegetables produced on the farm. The new husband of the ex-wife, who had been trying to run the farm, was a total failure. The herd of cattle had deteriorated, the land had become less productive, the farm mortgage had been increased, and a list of unpaid debts that were long overdue had accumulated and the bank was threatening to foreclose the mortgage for failure to meet interest and principal payments.

So what should be done?

If we held the ex-husband in contempt and committed him to jail, obviously all that would be accomplished would be to worsen an almost impossible situation. If in order to save himself from going to jail, he purged himself of contempt by making the four-dollars-a-week payments, then neither he nor his new wife and baby could possibly live on the remainder. Furthermore it certainly would be stretching things to an absurd length to hold under those circumstances that the ex-husband had *willfully* refused and neglected to pay the four dollars a week. The new wife and baby had to be taken care of somehow. The ex-wife and children also had to be provided for, and there was just not money enough to go around.

Before the evidence was all in, I was puzzling over what possible solution there could be. And then a novel idea struck me. The evidence had clearly shown that the ex-husband was a capable, industrious, and successful farmer. When the parties had been living together on the farm, the farm under his management had provided an adequate living for the family, and the land and the herd were improving each year. Surely, the ex-wife had made a bad mistake in swapping husbands.

So, at the conclusion of the presentation of evidence I called the lawyers into chambers. I told them that I was sure they would agree with me that there was no satisfactory solution to this case unless we employed bold and unorthodox methods. I told them I had in mind such a proposal, that it couldn't work without their cooperation and that of all the parties, including the new spouses. I frankly admitted that my proposal would have about one chance in ten of working, but since there was no other solution I was going to present the proposal. I proposed that a stipulation be signed by all parties upon the basis of which an order would be made as follows:

1. That the ex-husband should give up his present job and go to work for his ex-wife.

2. That he should be given living space on the farm in the 12-room house that constituted the homestead for his new wife and baby and himself.

3. That he should be paid $50 a month wages, in addition to receiving his firewood, milk, eggs, and vegetables from the farm.

4. That the new husband should give up working on the farm and find such work elsewhere as he could.

5. That the former order of four dollars a week should be canceled as long as this arrangement lasted.

6. That this arrangement should continue until further order of court and that either party was free to make application to the court at any time for cessation or amendment of the arrangement.

The lawyers, of course, were shocked by my proposal, which was what I expected. But, as our discussion continued and I pressed them to suggest a better solution, they began to be interested in the idea. Finally, it was agreed that the case should be continued for forty-eight hours, during which each attorney would discuss the proposal with his client.

When court convened two days later, counsel on both sides informed me that their clients would accept the proposal. Nearly half a day was then consumed in preparing the exact wording of the order and stipulation. The stipulation was signed by all the parties, and I signed the order.

Three years later, out of simple curiosity, I took occasion to investigate the situation. To my great joy, and to some extent my astonishment, I found that the parties were still living together on the farm in full harmony, and the farm showed clear signs of prosperity.

I have never quite dared to inquire since then.

Human Nature: A Tool for Justice

Vermont is, I believe, the only state that still has the institution of elected assistant judges in its Court of General Jurisdiction. They are provided for in our constitution, and despite many attempts to amend the constitution to eliminate this provision, it has remained the law. The assistant judges, commonly called side judges, are elected by the people in each county and hence, almost exclusively, are not lawyers. And yet, until some recent cases in the Vermont Supreme Court, which has by interpretation slightly narrowed their authority, they legally had the full equal authority in county court with the presiding judge. Thus the two nonlawyer side judges had and still have the power in factual situations to overrule the presiding judge. It has happened, although rarely.

I had a case while presiding Rutland County Court when the assistant judges nearly succeeded in overruling me. We were trying a contested divorce case. I was unaware that it was a cause célèbre and that there were strong political overtones. I became aware of it, however, as soon as the case was over and we had adjourned to the judges chambers to discuss what our decision would be. To me it seemed a clear case for the libelee. Since it did seem so clear, I thought surely that the two assistant judges would see it the same way. It became quite obvious to me that my distinguished associates were being unduly influenced by the political considerations involved, and I was determined that political considerations should not decide this case.

But what could a single judge, even if he was the presiding judge, do when he was outvoted by two judges who had the legal right to do so?

I decided to try human nature.

I knew that assistant judges have almost never, if ever, had occasion to draft findings-of-fact and judgment orders in a sharply contested case like this. Also, assistant judges are human and have pride, as do all of us.

So, when it appeared that agreement between us was impossible, I told them, "You constitute a majority of this court. Therefore your decision will be the decision of this court. So you draft your own findings-of-fact-and-judgment order and deliver them to me. But I want you to know that I am going to draft my own findings-and-judgment order and sign them. Not that they will have an effect on the ultimate judgment but I don't want posterity to think that I could be such a damn fool as to agree to what you are proposing to do." They said they would. I immediately drafted my own findings-of-fact-and-judgment order and told my associates that I was putting them in the drawer of the table in the judges room until they had theirs ready, and then we would file them with the clerk and direct appropriate entries at the same time.

Each morning I asked them if they had their findings and order drawn up. Their reply was always the same: they had not yet drafted them but would have them shortly. This went on every morning for a week. I knew that they would have to seek the help of some lawyer in order to do the job. I also gambled that their pride would not let them do so.

When we reassembled on Monday morning of the next week, I knew that my associates were in the building because their coats were hung in the closet but they were nowhere around. I entered the room and there on top of the table were *my* findings-of-fact-and-judgment order, duly signed by the two assistant judges.

Advice to a Young Judge

After dinner Judge Bicknell and I were sitting in the small lounge of the White Cupboard Inn in Woodstock, where Judge Bicknell was holding an extended session of Windsor County Court. It was October of 1931. I had just been appointed a superior judge and had decided to take a week of on the job training before taking up my new duties. I had, of course, watched presiding judges doing their job on the bench in hundreds of cases. But it had suddenly dawned on me that the perspective from the "bull pit," as we sometimes facetiously called the lower level of the courtroom where the lawyers operate, was quite different from the exalted level of the bench where the presiding judges sat and ruled over the case. And perspective means a lot.

So I had asked Judge Bicknell if he would let me sit with him on the bench for a week as an observer in the hope that I might gain additional knowledge and insight that would prove helpful in performing my new duties.

I had great admiration for Judge Bicknell, not only as a judge but in his former capacity as a trial lawyer in Windsor, where he had been a great success. I once asked him why he left his lucrative law practice to become a judge.

"Well," he said, "I practiced law for many years as you

know. But there came a time when if I heard steps coming up the stairs to my second-floor office I wanted to jump out the window. I decided it was time to quit."

That week with Judge Bicknell proved to be most helpful. I would certainly recommend a similar experience for any new trial judge.

So, at the end of the week as I was preparing to leave, I thanked Judge Bicknell for his help and then said, "Judge, you've taught me a lot in a short time. But haven't you just a few more parting words of wisdom as I go on my way?"

"Well," he said, "as a matter of fact I have. I've got three bits of advice that may help you more than anything you've learned this week."

"First, don't get yourself all in a sweat to try to make the lawyers get their cases tried on time. If one side presses for trial, then force the other side to trial unless there is substantial reason for delay. But you'll find that the majority of the cases that are never ready are the ones where both sides want them continued. Don't push the lawyers around. Usually there are good reasons not to try a case where both sides want the case continued. But the reasons are not the kind of reasons that get on the record. In those cases justice is just as likely to be done by not trying the case as it is if you force both sides to a trial neither wants.

"Second, when you rule on a question of law make your ruling as unmistakably clear as humanly possible. It's the cases where the Supreme Court can't figure out what you really meant by your ruling that justice often fails. Just remember you've got a fifty-fifty chance, at least, of being right. And if you make a mistake, the Supreme Court on appeal has another fifty-fifty chance of correcting your mistake.

"Third, at all times—and in all events—don't take yourself too damn seriously."

What Is Law?

The bell had just rung to signal the opening of the first lecture to the freshman class at Boston University Law School, of which I was a member. The first lecture was by Dean Homer Albers, dean of the law school and a recognized legal scholar as well as a practicing attorney. He was a lawyer's lawyer — meaning that all of his clients were lawyers who came to him for help in exceptionally complicated cases.

Dean Albers made a few general remarks and then said, "Now ladies and gentlemen, if you will get your notebooks open and your pens ready we will proceed. I think it might be well to start the lecture with a definition of what law is. Obediently, we opened our notebooks and waited for the words of wisdom to fall from the lips of this distinguished professor.

"Law, he said, "is something everyone is presumed to know." Dutifully we wrote down these words as fast as we could. "But which nobody in fact does know," he continued. Startled, the class hesitated, looked at each other in confusion. Dean Albers waiting patiently for those who with great uncertainty decided to write that down too. Then he concluded: "But for which the Supreme Court gets paid for having the last guess."

Experience has proven to me that there is more truth in those words than we lawyers like to admit.

A Stubborn Witness

Sitting on the bench in Rutland County Court toward the end
of a long and hotly contested divorce case, I was suddenly
brought face to face with a startling new situation as the last
witness, a sweet little old lady, was called to the stand. She
took the oath in a completely routine manner and looked as
harmless as anyone's favorite grandmother. Examining counsel began his interrogation in the usual way, by asking the
witness her name and residence, which she readily answered.

"Mrs. Scott," said counsel, "what is your age?"

"I don't want to tell you my age."

"Come, come, Mrs. Scott, surely there's no harm in telling
the court your age."

"But I don't want to. Why do I have to?"

"Because, Mrs. Scott, it is part of the necessary process of
identifying you as a witness," said counsel.

"But everybody can see me and I've already told you my
name and where I live. Why isn't that enough? I won't tell
you my age."

One could feel the tension mounting in the courtroom. At
this point it didn't take any great judicial acumen to know

that trouble was in the making. I silently prayed that counsel would have sense enough to drop it right there. But he didn't. He turned to me and said, "Your Honor, I suggest that the witness be ordered to answer the question." The fat was in the fire. By now this lady's stubborn refusal was spread all over her countenance and hardening rapidly. In the ordinary situation it would have been usual procedure to sternly admonish the lady and demand that she answer the question. But this was no ordinary situation. And, unless a confrontation were somehow avoided, I would be put in a situation of choosing to hold this witness in contempt of court or of having the court greatly embarrassed — neither of which options appealed to me in the slightest. So I turned and addressed the witness with the most conciliatory expression and tone of voice of which I was capable.

"Mrs. Scott, you do want to help the court in its task of administering justice, don't you?"

"Oh yes, of course."

"Now the age of a witness might sometimes become important as having some bearing on the witness's testimony, probably not in your case, but we never can tell until the case is concluded. Do you understand that, Mrs. Scott?"

"I think so but not very well," she answered.

"Now, Mrs. Scott, if you do tell your age and it goes on the record the only people who are likely to know are the people in the courtroom. And you can see there are only about twelve or fifteen people here."

"That's too many."

Increasing my conciliatory smile, I said, "The only ones that really need to know are myself and my two associate judges here. Don't you want to help us, Mrs. Scott?"

She hesitated a couple of moments, and then her sweet expression returned as she looked at me, smiled and said, "I'll tell you."

"I appreciate that, Mrs. Scott. So then why don't you come up here and tell me?"

She immediately descended from the witness chair, came around to the steps leading to the bench, approached me closely and whispered her age in my ear.

"Thank you, Mrs. Scott. The court appreciates your cooperation. You may resume the witness stand, and counsel may proceed with the interrogation."

If anyone had dared at that moment either to question the unorthodox procedure or even smile visibly I think I would have held him in contempt.

Reed Powell

One of the top constitutional lawyers of this country was former Vermonter Reed Powell. A distinguished professor of
constitutional law at Harvard Law School for many years, he
was born in Burlington, and some of the older lawyers will
remember that his brother operated a fine collection agency
there. He always treasured his Vermont birth and connection.

One year he was invited to be the principal speaker at the
prestigious dinner that marked the closing of the annual
meeting of the Vermont Bar Association. In those days a
large percentage of the active members of the bar attended
the two-day sessions.

On the day of the dinner I was quietly seated at my desk at
the National Life Insurance Company when the telephone
rang. It was the president of the association speaking from
the Pavilion Hotel, where the dinner was customarily held.
The president informed me that our distinguished guest had
arrived early and invited me to come up and help entertain
him until dinner time. Naturally, I accepted.

I had never met Reed Powell but had read much of the
legal literature he had produced and had the highest regard

for his legal and historical scholarship. Also, I knew of his high standing in the legal field and was most anxious to meet him.

Arriving at the Pavilion, I found four or five lawyers including the president and our guest having a hilarious time. The president introduced me to Powell, who shook hands and greeted me, "Oh yes, Deane Davis. I've heard of you. You're that kept lawyer down at National Life Insurance Company."

"That's right, professor, but you see I made up my mind that I'd rather be kept than promiscuous." This remark was not originally mine, but I was grateful that it popped into my memory at such a useful time.

With all his prestige and well-earned distinction, Powell was an individualist of the first order. He was most informal and indeed somewhat earthy, even on the most formal occasions. In those days the annual dinner was a most dignified occasion. The governor, the justices of the Supreme Court, and the superior judges always attended with their wives and graced the head table. The governor, the justices, the judges, and the officers of the bar association all wore dinner jackets and black tie, to add to the luster of the occasion. Even in this formal setting, Powell, during his forty-five-minute speech, smoked a cigar and consumed half a pint of whiskey. I have never seen that done before or since.

Although there was much of substance in the speech, it was liberally sprinkled with slightly off-color stories. A sample is the story of the West Virginia legislature in action. It seems that the legislature was considering a bill to raise the age of consent in statutory rape cases from 14 to 16. During the argument a legislator from the West Virginia hills arose and addressed the House as follows:

"Mr. Speaker, I just want to say that I have listened very

carefully to the arguments and I have made up my mind. I'm willing to vote to raise the age of consent from 14 to 16 — provided we make it compulsory from there on."

Long Terms for Judges

As long as I can remember, and I'm sure even longer than that, our method of electing both Supreme Court and superior judges has been unique in this country.

There are a variety of methods prevailing in the several states. Some are elected for life, some for long terms, some by the legislature, some by direct vote of the people. But none that I am aware of has as short a term as does a Vermont judge. Here the judges of those two courts are elected by the legislature every two years. If a vacancy occurs when the legislature is not in session, the governor appoints a judge to hold office until the next session of the legislature. In all cases, so far, the legislature has reelected the person appointed by the governor. Among lawyers there has always been a strong body of opinion favoring long terms for judges. Many even believe that appointment for life, as in the U.S. Supreme Court, is the best method—the reason being that long terms are thought to be a special safeguard against the possibility of judges being swayed by political influences and hence less judicial in their decisions.

Our method has worked well in Vermont. We have had no

known cases of corruption in our courts. And during the years I have known and observed the courts, there have been few, if any, cases of dictatorial or overbearing conduct on the part of judges. Hence there have been no real attempts to change the system. By tradition, the judges have been routinely reelected every two years by the legislature. And yet the fact that judges must run the gauntlet of legislative review each two years may be part of the reason for our outstanding judicial record.

At one of the annual dinners of the Vermont Bar Association, the principal speaker was Justice Pettingil, then chief justice of the Supreme Court of Maine. He took occasion to comment on the pros and cons of the various methods of electing judges then in vogue. When he came to the discussion of the Vermont system, he had this to say:

"Here in Vermont you have not only a system that is unique in all the country but one that is the best. For, as I have already made clear, I am wholeheartedly in support of long terms for judges. Now compare your system with ours in Maine. Yours are elected for a full term of two years. Whereas in Maine ours are only elected 'during good behavior.'"

A Generous Fee

Tony Bianchi was the owner of a large monumental manufacturing plant in the north end of Barre. He was a forceful, dynamic individual, with strong opinions and the will and ability to back them up. Along in middle age, Tony became afflicted with a severe case of arthritis, which grew progressively worse and finally made him a complete cripple.

Lester Cheyne was the owner and operator of a stationery and office-supply store in Barre. He ran for election as a member of the Barre City Council and was elected. He was appointed as chairman of the Police Committee, a post that pleased him because he was much interested in law enforcement. He entered into his duties as chairman immediately and gave it an unprecedented degree of personal attention. He was in almost daily touch with the police chief and supervised the policies and performance of the department with zeal. For some reason, a well-developed feud arose between Tony and Cheyne. The reason for the feud never became known, but the fact of its existence was widely known.

Late at night on a summer day, after Tony's arthritis had progressed to the point where he was using two canes, he drove his car onto Keith Avenue and parked it immediately opposite the back entrance to the Worthen block, which then housed the Elks Club on the second floor. Walking was extremely difficult for Tony, and he chose that spot to be as near the entrance as possible. Tony was on the way to the club for a bit of relaxation and companionship.

The spot where Tony parked his car was in a No Parking area. Tony ignored this because there was practically no traffic moving at that hour, and parking where he did would reduce the necessary steps to the entrance.

Lester Cheyne had been working late. As he came out of his store to go home, his course took him by Tony's car. Whether he recognized the car as belonging to Tony is not known. It was, however, a distinctive Cadillac that most people did recognize as Tony's. In any event, Cheyne saw the No Parking signs painted on the curb against which Tony's car was parked. He sprang into action immediately, drew a sheet of paper from his pocket, and wrote the following message and pinned it to the steering wheel of the Cadillac:

"Violation parking ordinance—Keith Ave. 10:45 p.m. Report to Police Station forthwith. (Signed) Police Committee. L.S."

Some time thereafter Tony came down the stairs from the club, entered his car, and noticed the note pinned to the wheel. He read it and drove immediately to the city police station. He greeted the officer on duty by asking, "Who put this d—— thing on my steering wheel?" The officer took the note, examined it carefully, and informed Tony that it was Lester Cheyne, chairman of the Aldermanic Police Committee.

"Well, you just tell Lester Cheyne to go jump in the lake." And simultaneously, he tore up the note into small pieces and threw the fragments into the wastebasket beside the officer's desk and hobbled out of the station. The next day, as instructed by Tony, the officer reported the incident and the conversation to Cheyne.

Thus the gauntlet was thrown down. In due course the city attorney, William Wishart, was instructed to prepare and serve a warrant for Tony charging him with violation of a city ordinance "against the peace and dignity of the state." Wishart had no recourse but to comply. He prepared the complaint and warrant and delivered it to the chief of police with instructions to bring Tony into court by serving the warrant.

The chief, a most genial person, knowing Tony and his reliability, instead of serving the warrant called Tony on the telephone at his plant office in the North End, a couple of miles from the police station, and suggested that Tony come up to the municipal court that day at his convenience to make his appearance.

"Chief," said Tony, "the law requires you to serve that warrant on me personally, doesn't it?"

"Yes," said the chief, "but I thought it would inconvenience you less if you came voluntarily to court."

"Well now, Chief, I appreciate your thoughtfulness, but if you want me you just better come and get me; and when you come be sure and bring that police wagon because I want everything legal."

The chief tried to talk Tony out of his position but to no avail. "Chief," said Tony, "I pay big taxes to help support you and that police wagon, and I want some service."

Finally, the chief came to the conclusion that Tony meant business, so he took the police wagon, drove to Tony's office, and presented his warrant for Tony's arrest. "Now Chief," said Tony, "the law requires you to read that warrant to me in order to make a legal arrest, doesn't it?"

"Yes," said the chief, "but I thought we could dispense with that in this case."

"Oh no," said Tony, "everything's got to be legal."

So the chief laboriously read the complaint with all its necessary legal jargon and also read the warrant directing his arrest.

"Now, that's good. I'm ready to go."

So up through the streets of Barre he was driven by the chief in the Black Maria, with Tony prominently seated in the front seat beside the chief. As they approached the center of town, Tony spied his friend William Wishart, who had issued the complaint. He directed the chief to pull over to the curb. Tony greeted his friend and directed him to get into the police wagon with them in the front seat. Wishart tried to demur, but Tony insisted and so Wishart climbed in and rode to the police station with its occupants.

In those days the municipal court was located directly above the police station. H. William Scott was the judge. All three went upstairs. The warrant was presented to the judge, and he made the necessary notations on the record, then turned to Tony and asked him if he pleaded guilty or not guilty. Tony replied, "Judge, in order to make that decision I will have to have the complaint read to me. I'm entitled to that, ain't I?" So the judge read the long complaint and again asked Tony if he would plead guilty or not guilty. Tony said, "Not guilty." The judge said, "I will fix bail at one hundred dollars and you may be released on your own recognizance."

"What does that mean, Judge?"

"It means that you won't have to get somebody to go bail for you," said the judge.

"Oh, no," said Tony, "everything must be in good legal form. Mr. Wishart will go bail for me. Won't you Bill?" A bit nonplussed, Wishart said, "Yes, yes, of course."

The chief then told Tony that he was free to go. "Oh, but you brought me up here in the police wagon, you're supposed to take me back where you found me." Thereupon an argument broke out as to whether Tony was entitled to this special service — an argument that Tony won in the end.

After arriving back at his office, Tony called me on the phone and asked if he could see me immediately. I told him he could, and in due course he arrived at my office.

"What can I do for you, Tony?"

"Want you to defend me against a criminal charge."

"You're kidding, Tony."

"Oh no, I'm not."

"Well, what's the charge?"

"Parking on Keith Avenue in a No Parking area."

"Did you do it?"

"Sure."

"Then what do you want me to do? Why don't you just go back up to court and plead guilty and pay a small fine? Probably not over five dollars fine and five dollars costs."

"Oh no," said Tony, "I want my rights. Doesn't the Constitution guarantee me a trial by jury?"

"It sure does, Tony. But that's a waste of time and money. You say you're guilty, what is there to try?"

"Well, the jury may not think I'm guilty. And in any event, I will have had my rights. Besides, Cheyne will have to testify, won't he?"

I tried my best to dissuade Tony, but he insisted he was going to have his "rights." So I told Tony that I would defend him, silently believing that if the case were continued for a bit Tony would come to his senses and plead guilty. So I embarked on a program of seeking successive continuances and had been able to put the case off about six weeks until finally Cheyne brought enough pressure on Wishart that he would agree to no more continuances. So we went into court and agreed upon a date assigned by the court for trial by jury.

I was quite disgusted with the whole performance by then. I thought, however, if I was going to do the impossible and defend Tony, I had better at least read the ordinance and the record of its passage. So I went to the city clerk's office and did so. I also checked the Vermont statutes under which authority municipalities had been granted the right to legislate local ordinances. There was a special section relating to parking ordinances. Immediately my interest was sparked.

The enabling statute after the granting language included a proviso. It was that in prohibiting parking in specified areas it was necessary to "post" signs prohibiting parking in clear and visual manner. In this case the No Parking signs were painted on the curb. A Supreme Court case was cited alongside the statute, and the finding in that case was that painting on the curb was not "posting." Posting, the case held, meant a sign "posted." So clearly the ordinance was invalid, and hence Tony could not be convicted. I immediately called Wishart and directed his attention to the Supreme Court decision in the case in question and suggested that he drop the prosecution. He demurred somewhat but said he would study the decision in the case and let me know. Shortly thereafter he called me and said he guessed I was right and that he would go into court the next day and drop the case against Tony. The next day, after he had done this, I called Tony and told him what had happened and why and told him the case was dropped.

"There," he said, "I told you that I was entitled to my rights. I'm glad you finally got around to do something for me instead of just trying to get me to plead guilty. I tell you our rights under the Constitution are very sacred and you lawyers better get busy and give people their rights. By the way, how much do I owe you?"

"You don't owe me anything, Tony. I didn't put in much time and really didn't do much for you. Forget it."

"Oh no," said Tony, "everything must be legal. I pay my bills."

"No, Tony. I won't send you a bill."

A few days later I was in consultation with a client in my private room in my law office when I heard a great commotion in the outer office. Loud voices indicated that Miss Cheever and Miss Tucker, the two secretaries in the outer office, were in violent argument with Tony trying to keep him out of my private office. Again Tony won.

In he came with his two canes and with him were two strong men from his plant bearing a heavy packing case. Tony directed them to put their burden down and uncrate it.

"I've come to pay you your fee," said Tony.

"I told you there was no fee."

"Oh yes, there's a fee. A good one, too. Course you didn't earn it. But it's a matter of principle with me. Four thousand dollars. Bet it's the biggest fee you ever were paid."

"Four thousand dollars! You're crazy, Tony."

"No, I'm not crazy. Just wait till you see it."

In due course the unpacking was accomplished. The object disclosed to view was a bronze bust of Teddy Roosevelt.

"You call that thing worth four thousand dollars?"

"Sure do. That's what it cost me. You see, I had an account of four thousand dollars due me from a granite dealer in Salem, Massachusetts, and he went into backruptcy and I got nothing. But a month after the bankruptcy he sent me this bust. So you see it's worth four thousand dollars, and it's without doubt the biggest fee you ever got for doing nothing."

Clients like Tony make country law practice a real joy.

The Duty to Inquire

Communication is a fascinating art — definitely not a science. Nowhere is this seen more often than in jury trials. Some lawyers are scholars and excel in research, in briefing, and in arguing cases in the Supreme Court. Others excel in the trial of jury cases, where the art of communication calls for different talents. Judge Fred Laird was an example of a good jury lawyer. He could read the minds of jurors and had a way of getting his points across that few possessed. It is not just one talent that makes this possible, it is a bundle of talents. Included in that bundle is the ability to pick and use a homely phrase at the right time, one that is within the range of experience of the particular jury being addressed, a phrase that has a special message all its own.

I am speaking from sad experience here. I was counsel for the Barre Trust Company in an action against Joseph Livingston to recover on a promissory note for twenty-five thousand dollars. The note had been given to and made payable to the Littlefield Piano Company, which ran into financial difficulties and later was declared bankrupt. The note was endorsed to the Barre Trust Company as collateral security for a new loan to the piano company.

George B. Littlefield, president of the Littlefield Piano Company, had approached Livingston, an old friend, for help in his financial troubles. He asked Livingston to sign a note that was made to the order of the piano company. Littlefield presented Livingston with a purported financial statement of the piano company, which grossly overstated the company's assets and surplus. Livingston was reassured by the financial statement and gladly consented to sign. He was told at the time that the note would be assigned to the Barre Trust Company and used for collateral security for a new loan. Eventually, the Littlefield Piano Company was declared bankrupt. The bank demanded payment from Livingston and when payment was not forthcoming brought suit to recover the twenty-five thousand dollars.

There was evidence that the bank had been loaning large sums of money to the piano company over a considerable period of time and knew intimately the piano company's precarious financial position.

The principal issue in the case was whether, at the time it took the Livingston note, the bank was "an innocent purchaser for value" of same. To be "an innocent purchaser for value," the bank had to prove that it had no knowledge of any defect in the Livingston note nor knowledge of any facts or circumstances that should have put the bank on notice of the possibility of some defect, and hence impose upon the bank the duty of making inquiry and investigation. The legal fraud inherent in the presentation of the overstated financial statement would be in the eyes of the law such a defect. For if the bank had made such inquiry it would have discovered the circumstances of the false financial statement and they would not be "innocent purchasers for value." So the issue really boiled down to whether the bank's intimate knowledge of the piano company's financial condition should have put it on notice.

Laird claimed in his argument that the bank was so involved with the piano company that they were desperately sending good money after bad in the hope of getting its money back and that this was the reason the bank made no inquiry as to the circumstances under which Livingston signed the note.

As Laird summed up with his usual consummate skill, he detailed the long list of loans made by the bank and argued that they were much larger than the piano company could ever be expected to pay. Then he reached the climax of his argument.

"Gentlemen of the jury," said Laird, "the bank didn't want to make inquiry as to the validity of that note. They were afraid of what they would find. And they wanted that additional security of Livingston's note to help them out of the hole they had dug for themselves. They just thought they had to stay on with Littlefield come hell or high water."

Here he paused, walked a few steps back to the counsel table, and then slowly turning to the jury, as though he had a new thought, concluded as follows:

"Gentlemen, when I was a small boy up on Maple Hill in Marshfield my father once gave me a bit of advice that is applicable here. He said to me, 'Freddie, don't never take hold of a hedgehog 'cause you can't let go.'"

The jury got his message.

Verdict for defendant Livingston.

Another Horse Trade

Harry Daniels of East Montpelier, a canny Vermonter, included among his many talents a shrewd ability to look after himself in a horse trade—or any kind of trade for that matter. A. Tomasi, who owned a large business block at the corner of North Main and Merchant Streets in Barre, was equally blessed with that talent.

A. Tomasi drove his sorrel mare over to East Montpelier in the hope of trading her off for a black mare that rumor had it was a marvelous animal that had just been shipped in from the West. The black mare was indeed a real looker. After an hour or two of sparring, a trade was finally consummated by the terms of which Tomasi was to pay Daniels one hundred dollars "to boot."

Tomasi started for Barre, happily driving his new black mare. Just after he turned toward Barre at the intersection of East Montpelier and the Barre Road, as he was passing the electric-car barn, his new horse collapsed and shortly expired. With the help of the volunteer crowd that gathered, arrangements were made for the disposal of the horse's body and for storing Tomasi's wagon and harness in the shed adjacent to

77

the electric-car barn. Tomasi boarded the next electric car for Barre.

By the time Tomasi arrived in Barre, several hours had elapsed from the time he had left Daniels's place in East Montpelier. Tomasi went immediately to the telephone and called Daniels. The conversation was as follows:

"Hello, Harry."

"Why, hello A."

"Harry, I just wanted to ask you a question."

"Yes, A. What did you want to know?"

"Harry, did you cash that check yet?"

"Why, yes, A., as a matter of fact I did. I had to go to Barre to do an errand so I took the check into the bank and cashed it."

"Thank you, Harry. Goodbye."

Good Reason

Roy Barnett was a successful dairy farmer and a leader in the Cooperative Marketing Movement, which meant so much to the farmers of Vermont in past years. He and I were in Boston on business connected with one of the Vermont Cooperative organizations for which I served as counsel.

We had breakfast in the dining room of the hotel where we were staying. Our waitress was clearly "out of sorts." She wore a grim expression, was surly in her conversation, banged the dishes around unnecessarily, and clearly showed that for her the world was not a happy place.

When she had finally taken our orders and started for the kitchen I said to Roy, "What in the world do you think is the matter with her?"

His reply was prompt, brief, and to the point. "Simple," he said, "poorly stayed with."

Choice of a Candidate

In one county of Vermont two lawyers were running for the office of state's attorney — Boutwell and Harrington. Joseph Renfrew knew them both but couldn't make up his mind which man to vote for. He went to see his friend, Walter Condon, who was a kind of father confessor for the neighborhood in many things, including things political.

"Who shall I vote for, Walt?"

"Well, I tell you, Joe, if I had lost my pocketbook with a lot of money in it I would rather send Boutwell after it. But if I was in trouble, in a real mess, I would rather go to Harrington to get me out. You make up your mind."

A Canny Cop

John Maloney was a much loved member of the Barre police force. He was a good and loyal patrolman. And, in the rough and tumble situations that often occurred in those days, he had an unusual talent. But nobody, not even he, claimed that his intellectual level was particularly high. An incident that occurred on the job will illustrate this point.

Having arrested a man in North Barre, he was leading him to the jail, which was a considerable distance toward the south of the city. As they passed Martin's Book Store on North Main Street, the prisoner said, "Wait a minute will you, officer, I want to go into the store and buy a newspaper."

"Oh, no you don't, me lad," said Officer Maloney. "You stay here and I'll go in and get the newspaper myself."

No Recourse

Joe's Bar, located on the corner of the two principal streets of one Vermont town, was the popular gathering place for those who, lacking anything better to do, liked to spend their evenings in congenial if not always stimulating companionship. There the current news and gossip was communicated and thoroughly discussed and analyzed. If you were campaigning for political office, as I was at the time, you had just better make a stop there or, if possible, several stops. Bars of this sort in Vermont have replaced the country store as the locus for dispensing news, gossip, and wisdom.

Peter, local handyman, had a well-developed and quite persistent thirst. This made it difficult for him to keep his bills paid on time. He soon developed a county-wide reputation for being a deadbeat.

Joe, the proprietor, supervised his two bartenders from his "office" in a far corner of the room. His office consisted of a somewhat dilapidated chair and an ancient rolltop desk.

One night Peter came into the bar, stepped up to the bartender, and asked for a drink, which was promptly served and consumed. Then Peter said, "Can I be trusted for this?"

The bartender shouted across the din of the room to his boss, "Hey, Joe, Peter wants to be trusted for a drink."

Joe shouted back, " 'as he 'ad it?"

"Yes."

"Yes."

Literal Compliance

My father, also a country lawyer, had for many years owned the family farm, where he was born, on Pike Hill in the town of Corinth. He leased it to various individuals, sometimes on a sharecrop basis and sometimes for specified annual rent. One of these tenants was Harold Wheeler, a confirmed Vermonter.

Because most of the milk produced in Vermont was shipped into the Boston milk market for human consumption, the Massachusetts Department of Health maintained vigorous regulation and inspection of the conditions under which milk was produced in Vermont. They issued regulations from time to time and periodically sent inspectors into Vermont to observe on the scene just exactly what conditions were. Most of these regulations were based on common sense and were clearly conducive to protecting the health of the consuming public in Massachusetts and surrounding areas. But, like most bureaucratic regulation, they would occasionally invoke regulations that were quite impractical.

One of the new regulations passed was to the effect that farmers could no longer cool their milk by immersing the containers in a watering tub to which animals had access.

It had been customary for a long time for farmers to put the warm milk taken from the cows into thirty-quart cans and immerse them in the barnyard watering tub while waiting for the milk to be picked up for shipment by the milk truck. Various means were used to protect the cans from being overturned or molested in any way by the animals while drinking. One of the most common was to so construct the tub that the barnyard fence ran right through and over the middle of the tub, and the cans were placed on the outside of the barnyard where they were protected and also easily available to the trucker.

Wheeler paid no attention to the new regulation. The evidence is not clear as to whether he knew of the new regulation or whether, with characteristic Vermont independence, he chose to ignore what he considered an unnecessary and foolish regulation. Shortly after the inauguration of the new regulation, an inspector from Massachusetts visited the farm. Wheeler's practices passed the test with the exception of his facilities for cooling the milk. The inspector told Wheeler that he would have to refuse certification of his milk for the Boston market. This was of course a disaster for Wheeler because it meant that the milk could not be marketed anywhere and would have to be thrown away.

"What can I do?" said Wheeler.

"Well, you buy an electric milk cooler, get a bill of sale from the dealer, and send it to me at this address in Boston and I will recertify you," said the inspector.

That very day Wheeler drove to Hardwick and purchased from the Daniels Manufacturing Company an electric milk cooler on the installment plan. On the way back he mailed the bill of sale to the place specified, took the milk cooler home, and placed it in the woodshed and continued to cool his milk in the old-fashioned way. Within a few days the recertification came through from Boston, and for at least five years, to my knowledge, he continued cooling the milk as before and continued shipping his milk to the Boston market.

You see, during that time the inspector had overlooked the fact that there was no electric line into that portion of Pike Hill and hence no electricity available to run a milk cooler.

Sweet Wind

Mrs. Avery, a widow living on a back farm outside the village of Cookville, eked out a marginal existence mainly by keeping a few cows and hens, supplemented by occasional opportunities to do temporary housework in case of illness in the family or other unusual events. Her only help in running the farm was her fourteen-year-old son, Alton, who had been born on the farm and who, like most Vermont farm boys, filled a man's shoes at an extremely early age.

Mrs. Avery and her son were closely confined to the farm and did little traveling. They had, of course, visited the villages in the several townships adjacent to Cookville, but they had never been to Barre City, some twenty miles away. To them Barre seemed a faraway big city. Then came the day they were offered a ride to Barre by a neighbor, and amid much excitement they decided to accept. One of the items on their agenda was to have an ice cream soda, a privilege neither of them had ever experienced but one which had been highly recommended by another neighbor.

So the big day came, and they made the trip. Eventually they were directed to Drown's Drug Store, which maintained and operated a soda fountain.

Both were a bit timid about ordering an ice cream soda, but after much consultation of the menu, of each other, and of the soda fountain clerk, they settled on a chocolate ice cream soda. It was served, as is customary, with both a spoon and a straw. This was a bit confusing. Neither were sure which was to be used — the spoon or the straw. After discussing the problem for a few moments, Alton boldly tackled the straw while his mother looked on. Alton glanced up at his mother with a surprised and pleased look on his face and said:

"Gee, Ma, it's just sweet wind."

To Grasp an Opportunity

Many years ago it was fairly common practice in Vermont for funerals to be conducted without benefit of clergy, particularly in the most rural areas. The service would consist of appropriate music and reading of the scripture by some volunteer. Following which, upon invitation from the mortician, a few friends would relate an incident involving the deceased or deliver short words of eulogy.

On one such occasion a funeral was taking place in the backroad section of Calais. After the music and the reading of scripture, the mortician asked, "Would anyone like to say a few words on behalf of the deceased?"

There was a long, embarrassing silence. Finally, a gentleman in the back seat arose and said, "Mr. Smith, if no one cares to talk on behalf of the deceased I would like to take this opportunity to say a few words on behalf of the Republican Party."

Vermont Salesmanship

John Cummings had owned and operated a farm on East Hill in Barre Town for many years. He was a hard working, industrious, successful farmer and completely honest. But he was most direct and curt in his conversation.

Came the day, as it does to us all, when he knew he must retire. It was a most reluctant decision. He loved the farm, and selling it was almost more than he could bear.

He placed an advertisement in the *Barre Daily Times*. Almost immediately, Donald Tetzlaf, an associate of mine at National Life Insurance Company, noticed the ad and called Cummings on the phone. This was on Friday night. The conversation went like this.

"Hello, Mr. Cummings?"

"Yup."

"I read in the *Barre Times* that your farm is for sale."

"Yup."

"How many acres in the farm, Mr. Cummings?"

"Don't know. Never measured it."

"Well, then, how many cows can it carry?"

"More'n you'd want to milk."

"Is the house in good condition?"

"Suits me."

"How about the barn?"

"That don't suit me."

"Well, Mr. Cummings, I'd like to see the farm. Are you going to be there tomorrow?"

"No. But the farm will."

Great Expectations

John Slayton was an agent for National Life Insurance Company and was attached to the Boston agency. Calvin Coolidge was then governor of Massachusetts. Slayton had met the governor in connection with alumni activities of Amherst College and decided to use that connection to help him sell a life insurance policy to the governor. He finally succeeded in getting an interview with the governor in the governor's office at the statehouse. Slayton had planned his approach very carefully. He designed a very ambitious and most professional estate plan for the governor. He presented it thoroughly and skillfully, but he had difficulty in getting the governor to respond during the presentation, which is not very helpful to a salesman. Finally, when Slayton could find nothing more to say, he paused, sat back, and waited to learn his fate.

The governor said, "Yes, you've made a good presentation. I will buy one of your policies." Greatly elated, Slayton pulled an application form from his brief case and proceeded to fill in the required information. He left unfilled, until the last minute, the blank that would indicate the size of the policy applied for. Finally, with some hesitation but with great anticipation, he inquired of the governor as to the amount of the policy he would apply for. Slayton had visions of something around 50,000 dollars. The governor was silent for a few minutes, apparently pondering the question. As the silence continued, Slayton's expectations soared to something around 100,000.

Finally the governor said, "Well, I think a thousand dollars will be adequate." Slayton was crushed. But he knew at this point it would be useless to attempt to change the governor's mind. One well-known characteristic of the governor was that he did his own thinking; made up his own mind, and when it was made up it was final. So Slayton completed the application, secured the governor's signature and then inquired, "Governor, when would you be able to be examined?"

"Oh, I have to be examined?"

"Yes."

"How much does that cost?"

"Well, it costs five dollars but the company pays for that," said Slayton.

"Well, let's see. In May I have to go up to Montpelier to address a meeting of the Vermont Historical Society at the Pavilion. I'll go into the company's home office and let one of the doctors there examine me and that will save the company five dollars."

And he did. And he brought with him his father, John Coolidge, then living in Plymouth. Dr. Colton, who was then National Life Medical Examiner, told me that was a big day for National Life. Those at the home office were greatly impressed with both the governor and his father.

Pure Air

When I was campaigning for a second term as governor of Vermont, I pulled into the village of Calais where I met by prearrangement approximately twenty or twenty-five voters. After making a few informal remarks, I asked if there were any questions. At about that time there was much discussion in the news media about the matter of clean air in Vermont. One resident arose and said:

"Governor, what about all this clean-air discussion we hear about? Have we got a problem in Vermont with clean air?"

I responded with a short dissertation of my views, which included a statement that we would have a problem if we didn't have a clear state policy on the subject soon. As soon as I concluded, he arose again and said:

"Well, Governor, thank you. But you know it's hard to believe we can have a problem with clean air in Vermont. Why, up here in Calais, we got air that ain't never been breathed."

I still don't know whether he was serious or pulling my leg.

Privacy

Years ago, Anton Goodrich was a realtor in the town of Elmore. Goodrich was a successful operator and knew values of real estate with the best of them. He often bought real estate that came on the market and held it until a customer came along.

One year he bought a small house and barn on a dead-end road in a most remote section of the town; the road was nearly impassable.

His friend, Bradley Thomas, asked him, "Anton, why in the world did you buy that place? It's way out of sight, and a poor road to it, no view, and not in too good condition. Who in the world would be interested in that place?"

"Oh," said Anton, "it would be a great place for a single man and his wife."

All There

Charlie Slayton, a very deliberate individual, had a check to cash and went into his bank in Northfield just a minute or two before closing time and presented his check for 200 dollars. As his turn finally came up at the cashier's station, there were several people in line right behind him. It was now ten minutes past closing time, and everybody was a bit impatient and irritated. The cashier counted out ten 20-dollar bills and passed them over to Slayton. Slayton fingered it a bit slowly and then said:

"I kinda wanted that in 5-dollar bills."

With a clearly disgusted expression, the cashier took the 20-dollar bills back and counted out forty 5-dollar bills. Slayton picked them up slowly and then even more slowly and deliberately counted them.

The cashier, whose annoyance was visibly increasing, said in a sarcastic tone, "Well, Mr. Slayton, is it all there?"

"Just barely," said Slayton.

Good Security

One of the stories that had a persistent circulation in the 1930s involved Joe Hood, a Vermont farmer who applied for a loan at a Northfield bank. I have always thought that stories that persist over long periods of time are either true, partly true, or at least characteristic of the people and their times. This one, I believe, does characterize the Vermonter of the early 1930s. He was a canny individual and expected everybody to look out for himself. And he lived by his own precepts. He was extremely careful with money—and for good reason: there was so little of it, and he couldn't afford to lose it. He was suspicious enough of people in general that caution in dealing with them was second nature to him.

Mr. Hood, a rather unsuccessful farmer, came into the bank seeking to borrow 5,000 dollars. He was interviewed in the private office of Harold Moore, vice-president and one of the loan officers.

"What security have you got, Joe?"

"Well, my farm and cattle," answered Joe.

"Tell me about your farm. How many acres are there? And what kind of land is it?"

"There are 150 acres. Twenty acres of hay land, and the rest is swamp, pasture, and woods."

"What is the pasture land like?"

"Well, its pretty rocky and thin soil. I have to rent pasture in addition to keep my cows."

"What condition are the buildings in?"

"Oh, I'd say fair. Suit me. The house needs a new roof, and the chimney needs rebuilding. The porch sags some, and the underpinning is rotted on one side. Oh yes, it needs painting. But other than that it's quite comfortable."

"How about the barn?"

"Well, lightning struck one end of the roof. I ain't got around to fix it yet. One part of the floor on the south end has fallen in, but I figure I can do most of the work and fix that myself."

"How about your cows?"

"There's twenty of them. They haven't been tested for Bangs Disease yet. Five of them were barren last year. I gotta get rid of them, but I have been waiting for the price of beef to rise. Anymore I can tell you?" said Joe.

"No, I guess not," said Moore.

"Well then, Mr. Moore, what are you going to do? All I want to know is, do I get the loan? I don't want a lot of banker doubletalk. Just tell me yes or no."

"O.K.," said Moore, "the answer is no."

"Thank you," said Hood, and he left Moore's office.

A little later Moore came out of his private office and noticed Hood standing at the cashier's window, apparently depositing money. Curious, he investigated and found that Hood had just deposited 5,000 dollars in a savings account. When Hood left the window, Moore accosted him.

"Joe, what in the world is the idea? Here you are depositing 5,000 dollars, and a few minutes ago you were trying to borrow 5,000."

"Well, you see, Mr. Moore, it's like this. I just received 5,000 dollars that my uncle left me and I been wondering where to put it. So I thought I'd check up on this bank. When you told me right off you wouldn't make that loan on my security, I was pretty sure my money would be safe here."

Too Late

On one Saturday night the customary hangers-on at the country store in Calais had sat later than usual getting caught up on the news, the politics, and current gossip. At ten o'clock the grandfather's clock on the shelf started to strike. It was out of order and quite undependable. It struck eighteen times.

Sam Baldwin, who had been dozing in his chair, came fully awake with a start.

"Gee, boys," he said, "guess I'll git along. This is the latest I ever knew it to git."

Remembered

George Hoyt was born and grew up in Chelsea in the horse-and-buggy days. He, like many others of his age group, left Vermont on reaching his majority, seeking greater opportunities. Hoyt went to Iowa and eventually by hard work and Yankee ingenuity became a successful businessman. Then he ran for Congress from his Iowa congressional district. Although he had not returned to Chelsea in more than twenty-five years, he was proud of his Vermont heritage and finally decided to make a visit to his hometown.

He came into Barre by train and took the only public conveyance then available to get to Chelsea. This was the horse-drawn stage that carried the mail to Washington and Chelsea. He was the only passenger, so he was soon engaged in conversation with the driver.

"Do you know who I am?" he asked, addressing the driver.

"Oh yes."

"You know I was born in Chelsea?"

"Oh yes."

"Do people in Chelsea remember me?"

"Oh yes."

"Do they still talk about me?"

"Oh yes."

"Do they know that I was elected to Congress?"

"Oh yes."

"Well, what did they say when they heard?"

"Oh, they just laughed."

An Alert Nurse

On one of my hospital experiences I was being cared for in the intensive-care unit of Central Vermont Medical Center at Berlin. After a short stay I was soon to be discharged. One of the very attractive nurses among the staff there was quite conversational. I learned from her that she had recently moved to Vermont from Connecticut. On one afternoon, when I was the only patient left in the unit and there was little to do, she came to my bedside and we chatted about a number of things. Then she asked me, "Mr. Davis, what is your business?"

"Well," I said, "I'm retired."

"What did you do before you retired?"

"Oh, I've done a variety of things."

"Well, like what?" she asked.

"Well," I said, "I used to practice law; later I was on the bench; and then I was general counsel of the National Life Insurance Company and later its president. After that I served two terms as governor of Vermont."

Quick as a bunny she left me and went over to the nurse's station. I was puzzled and wondered if I had in some way offended. Later I learned what had happened. She told the head nurse:

"We ought to take Mr. Davis's temperature. I think he is delirious—he thinks he was governor of Vermont!"

Unnecessary Expense

Vermonters are often accused of being pinch pennies – an unjust accusation in my experience. However, there never was quite enough money in the early days of Vermont. And Vermonters in those days did live within their incomes. Doubtless that is the basis for the accusation.

Joe Templeton met his friend, George Wallace, on the street of a small Vermont town. George said:

"I hear you got married last week, Joe?"

"That's right."

"Where did you go on your honeymoon?"

"Niagara Falls."

"Did you enjoy it?"

"You bet."

"Did your wife enjoy it?"

"Well, she didn't go."

"Didn't go!"

"No. She'd been to Niagara Falls."

A Fair Price

Chauncey Willey was president of the Quarry Savings Bank and Trust Company in Barre. He was a warmhearted individual who, in addition to being a good banker, tried to help the bank's customers in any problem whenever they called on him for advice. He was an excellent example of the country banker. He had many clients and a wide range of situations with which to deal.

One of the bank's customers was Miss Lillie Sanborn, a schoolteacher from Hartford, Connecticut, who loved the country and had purchased a small house and a few acres of land outside the village of Washington, Vermont. She came there to spend the whole summer each year.

She had trouble disposing of her garbage, and a neighbor advised her to get a pig. So she called her valued friend and reliable adviser, Chauncey Willey, and asked him how to go about securing a pig. In his usual helpful manner Willey told her he would find one for her. He called one of his farmer customers who raised pigs to sell and asked him to deliver one to Miss Sanborn. The farmer was glad to comply and delivered one about six weeks old for which he charged Miss Sanborn

the modest price of fifteen dollars.

Miss Sanborn thoroughly enjoyed her pig all summer. She babied it, loved it, and fed it extra well. The pig flourished under her tender loving care and by the end of the summer weighed more than 200 pounds. Now she must return to school duties and there could be no pig in her life in Hartford. Reluctantly and sorrowfully, she again called Willey for advice on how to dispose of the pig. Chauncey told her he would handle the transaction for her and asked her how much she thought she ought to get for the pig.

"Well," she said, "I don't know much about the market price for pigs. Let's see. I paid fifteen dollars for her. But of course I've had the use of her all summer. Do you think ten dollars would be asking too much?"

Try Again

Few people in Vermont remember the old disclosure law, which prevailed in Vermont for many years. The reasons for its original enactment are lost in the dim recesses of past legislative history. The statute provided in those days that any person convicted of intoxication should be brought before a magistrate and be required, under oath, to disclose where he obtained the liquor that had caused his intoxication. Most of these people were alcoholics and upon being arrested for intoxication were lodged in jail to sober up and then brought into court, charged with being intoxicated. So widespread was the practice of arrests for intoxication that in the winter many hopeless alcoholics would choose the jail where they would like to be incarcerated based on the quality of the "service" and the food provided by the jailer. In the coldest weather they hoped to be sentenced for at least sixty days, during which time they could live in warmth and comfort. Today, arrests for simple intoxication are rare indeed.

When brought into court after sobering up, these people became most adept at dreaming up stories to satisfy the magistrate without disclosing the true source of their supply.

And one of the factors to be considered in selecting the place to get arrested was the leniency or lack of it in the local magistrate, as to his willingness to accept obvious fabrications concerning where the accused got his supply. If it was in the winter the alcoholic wanted a judge who was quite strict in order to be sure of a good long sentence, long enough to outlast the worst of the winter weather. At other times of the year the alcoholic would prefer a lenient magistrate so that an obvious untruth would be accepted automatically.

John Senter, one of Vermont's distinguished trial lawyers of those days, was pinch-hitting for the judge of the municipal court in Montpelier, who was away on vacation. He was holding court in the county clerk's office, having borrowed the room for his own convenience in trying to dispose of some routine pending matters. Senter, though temporarily acting as a judge, was quite informal. He sat with his feet on the desk in front of him while he proceeded to carry out his official duties.

A habitual offender, arrested the night before and kept in jail until morning, was brought before Senter for arraignment. He promptly pleaded guilty, which most alcoholics did. Pursuant to law, Senter put him under oath and asked him to disclose where he got the liquor that caused his intoxication. It was spring, and the accused hoped and believed that he had a lenient judge, because Senter had a reputation of being a heavy drinker himself.

"Well you see, Judge, I was walking down the railroad tracks in the Central Vermont freight yard late at night and suddenly I saw an empty freight car with the door open. And there right in the door of the car on the floor was a pint of whiskey. And that's how I got drunk."

The accused saw immediately that he had misread his judge. Bringing his feet down off the desk and slamming them on the floor, Senter pounded on the table and addressed the accused as follows:

"Now this court has drank altogether too much booze to believe any such cock-and-bull story as that. You are hereby remanded to Washington County Jail until you can think up a better lie than that."

Gratitude

Arthur Charlton was a big, strong-shouldered, hard-muscled man of 250 pounds who owned and operated a dairy farm on East Hill in Barre Town. He also worked as a blacksmith for one of the granite manufacturing companies in Barre City.

He was triply blessed with his wife. She was a very small woman, weighing just about 100 pounds. She had borne and reared 11 children. In addition to keeping her home immaculate and looking after the needs of her children, she helped with the milking, rode the tractor, the mowing machine, and the hay rake, and even helped in pitching hay during haying season. Her incredible energy and drive for such a small woman was one of the wonders of the East Hill community. Finally, she became ill and died.

Shortly after her death, Charlton was in the People's National Bank in Barre to conduct some routine bank business. Barrett Nichols, executive vice-president and manager of the bank, noticed him and walked over to express his condolences.

"Thank you, Mr. Nichols. Yes. You're right. She was a good woman. But a little light for my business."

A Little River

Many stories were told about Harry Daniels of East Montpelier. He was a many-sided personality. One of the most energetic and active men I ever knew, he often became impatient at the speed or lack of it with which things moved around him. Nowhere was this more evident than in the Vermont Senate, where he served several terms.

The Senate was debating a bill to change the name of a river in the northeastern part of the state. The debate had been in process for nearly an hour, and Harry was becoming more impatient by the minute, partly, perhaps, because a favorite bill of his was scheduled to come up for action immediately following. Finally, he could stand it no longer. He rose and addressed the Senate as follows:

"Mr. President, it seems to me we're spending altogether too much time on a matter of little importance. I wonder how many members of the Senate know how small this so-called river is. I know it well. Why, I could spit halfway across that damn river."

Thereupon the presiding officer of the Senate interrupted. "Senator," he said, "you're out of order."

"I know I am, Mr. President," said Harry, "and if I wasn't I could spit clear across."

Summer Folks

Walter Hard, Sr., of Manchester, Vermont, father of long-time editor of *Vermont Life,* Walter Hard, Jr., was a widely known Vermonter who wrote both prose and poetry. He had a great talent for accurately portraying Vermonters in prose and verse with unusual perception. He operated a bookstore in Manchester, one of the most beautiful villages in Vermont. A number of legendary tales about him have circulated widely in Vermont.

One that was illustrative of his wry humor and quick wit involved a Harvard professor who spent the summer in Manchester writing a book. In view of their common literary interests, it was only natural that the professor should come to know Walter Hard. They became good friends.

At the end of the summer, as the professor was preparing to return to his duties at Harvard, he came into Hard's store to bid his friend good-bye.

"How did you like Vermont, professor?"

"Oh I think it is a great place. Beautiful and quiet. But you've got to admit there's a lot of queer people up here."

"Yes. That's right," said Hard, "but they all go home come September.

An Obedient Client

John Senter has been mentioned previously. He lived and practiced law in Montpelier and was a legal scholar of the old school. In the latter part of his life he had earned and enjoyed a reputation for legal ability that was widely known and much to be envied. He became a lawyer's lawyer. A large proportion of his clients were lawyers who consulted him when they had an unusual or complicated case. I well remember, as a teenager, driving with my father in the family buggy from Barre to Montpelier to consult Senter. At that time he lived in a suite of rooms over what is now the Lobster Pot Restaurant. Joseph Frattini, later to become the clerk of Washington County Court and of the Supreme Court, functioned as a law student, clerk, errand boy, valet, and nurse for Senter since Senter's health was not good at the time.

Scholar though he was, he was at times an impulsive character. Sam Jones, his client, was having legal difficulties with a neighbor regarding water rights to a spring. Sam came in to see Senter almost daily to report some minor bit of gossip or some incident connected with the controversy. This annoyed Senter.

114

One day Jones came in to tell his lawyer that he had just heard a rumor circulating in East Montpelier that his neighbor Brown was going to cut the pipe leading from the spring to Jones's house.

"If he does," said Jones, "what shall I do, Mr. Senter?"

Annoyed, Senter said, "Shoot the b-----d!"

About a week later, Senter received a telephone call from the sheriff at the county jail, advising him that Sam Jones was in jail and wanted to see him. Senter went over to the jail to see what this was all about. He asked Jones what was he in jail for.

"For shooting my neighbor Brown."

"Aghast, Senter said, "My God, did you do that?"

"Yes, I did."

"What in the world made you do that?"

"Don't you remember? You told me if Brown cut my pipe to shoot him. Well, he did cut it and I did what you told me to do."

Luckily, the victim was shot in the leg and recovered easily. The record does not show how Jones came out on the charge for assault.

The Devil Himself Knows Not the Mind of Man

Judge Harland B. Howe did not believe in what he called "settling lawyers." He believed in "fighting lawyers." I remember riding with him on the train one Sunday afternoon. We were on our way to Brattleboro, where each of us was to hold court—he in that beautiful movie set federal courtroom in Brattleboro, and I in the ancient but equally beautiful courthouse at Newfane.

It was always a pleasure to chat with Judge Howe. He was quite opinionated, and so was I. We enjoyed sparring with each other and usually disagreed more often than we agreed, which always makes for interesting conversation.

He said, "You know, I'm getting tired of this judging business. If I can be sure of getting a Democrat for a successor, and if I can get my wife's consent, and if I can get up my own courage, I'm going to resign this judging job and I'm going back to practicing law. And I'm not going to be one of those ———— settling lawyers. I'm going to be a fighting lawyer." This remark brought on a heated discussion between us concerning settlements in the administration of civil justice.

His thesis was that once a case was brought there should

be no compromise settlement, that true justice was best accomplished by going through to the bitter end of the trial and letting the court decide the case. We disagreed on this, too. I like fighting lawyers. And fighting lawyers, those with the ability and will for combat, usually do the best job for a client. And yet, justice is not an exact science. Usually there are more than two sides to a case. As I have often said, there are three sides. Your side, my side, and the right side. And the elusive thing is to define exactly what is that right side. Hence it is my opinion that in almost every case counsel should carefully weigh the question as to whether the interests of his client could best be advanced by a compromise settlement. If the answer is no, or if the other side is not interested in settlement, then I believe one should fight with every honorable weapon at hand.

I asked the judge, "But suppose you get an offer of settlement from the other side and your client wants to take it?"

"Don't tell your client."

That, of course, would be highly improper conduct on the part of an attorney. And I'm sure the judge did not really mean it. He was only using colorful language to dramatize his belief in "fighting lawyers."

The case I am describing here is a good example of how compromise settlements are sometimes the best service a lawyer can render to his client.

In will cases the intent of the testator is the key question. It's surprising how many times that intent is difficult to determine. Usually these cases are a question of determining intent from unclear wording. But often, too, intent becomes an issue when it is not clear whether or not the testator intended to revoke his will. In Vermont, as in most parts of the United States, a will may be revoked by a clear and unequivocal act of destruction or mutilation of a written will, such as burning, tearing, or a similar act coupled with circumstances from which it may be inferred that revocation was indeed the testator's intent. But sometimes there are no surrounding circumstances. And the question must be decided by the nature of the physical act performed on the will.

I remember well, as a teenager, attending with my father a hearing before the probate judge of Orange County in the case of Orton Smith's will. The case was heard in the back room of the Hastings Store in Cookville in the town of Corinth. Smith was a miser in the full sense of the word. He hoarded everything, and his place looked like a cross between a junkyard and a menagerie. He kept sheep and carefully sheared them each year. Instead of selling the wool he packed it in bales and stored it under a shed waiting for a higher price. And in a sense he was vindicated. The hearing was being held during the middle of World War I, and the price of wool had soared to an extremely high level. Smith, in addition to the wool, livestock, farm machinery, and his small farm, owned about 500 acres of land on Pike Hill adjoining my grandfather's farm, and in addition he had savings accounts totaling around 50,000 dollars.

The will that was found in the drawer of an old desk in his house had been literally cut, apparently with shears, clear across. All of the words of the will were clearly legible. None of them had been touched by the incision. The will purported to leave all the testator's property to Dartmouth College. Homer Skeels, then of Ludlow, connected with the prestigious firm of Stickney, Sargent and Skeels, represented Dartmouth College, and my father represented two aged ladies who were cousins of the testator and the only next of kin. If the will was valid, Dartmouth College would take all. If the will had been revoked, the two cousins would take all.

Skeels offered the will for probate. My father objected to

118

its allowance on the ground that it had been revoked by the testator by the mutilation described. Not a single word of evidence was offered one way or the other as to intent other than what might be inferred from the act of cutting the will. But, alas, there was no evidence as to who had cut the will. Was it done by the testator or by accident or design by someone else?

So — if you were the judge, what would you do? Or, if you were the parties in interest or the lawyers, what would you do?

Surely, here we had a case with fertile ground for long litigation involving extensive investigation in the neighborhood, then through trial in county court and on appeal to the Supreme Court. Fortunately, the two lawyers were more interested in doing the best they could for their respective clients. Years of litigation and great expense might leave little of the estate left in the end.

So, in due course, they sat down and agreed upon the terms of a settlement that would be proposed to clients on both sides. The proposal would in effect divide the estate on a fifty-fifty basis. The proposition was accepted on both sides, and everybody was happy. Yes, settling lawyers have their proper place in the system of administration of justice.

Estimate by Formula

Henry Perkins, a summer resident, had a cottage on a small lake. His water supply from a surface spring had become quite temperamental, and he decided to explore the feasibility and cost of drilling an artesian well. He sent for Joseph Drummond, who was engaged in the business of drilling artesian wells in the same county. Perkins showed Drummond around his place and explained his problem. After looking the situation over, Drummond told Perkins it was entirely feasible to put in an artesian well and that he would be glad to do the work.

"How much will it cost?" asked Perkins.

"Eight dollars a foot."

"Now is there some way to estimate the number of feet you would have to go down to get water? Don't you have some formula based on the contour of the land or other physical characteristics or visual objects?"

"Sure. We have a formula. But it isn't based on the contour of the land or anything like that."

"Well, what is your formula?"

"Well, it's comparatively simple. It's like this. In this

county the number of feet we have to go down is usually between 125 and 150 feet. So if your customer is just an average citizen we estimate between 125 and 150. But if our customer is some high-hat rich s.o.b. we usually estimate 300 feet."

Too Many Husbands

In most states the marriage laws require that some kind of ceremony be performed before the parties will be recognized as husband and wife. There are a few states, however, in which the ancient doctrine of common law marriage is still recognized and under which no ceremony or public record is required to effect a legal and valid marriage. This doctrine was inherited by those states which accepted it as part of the common law of England. Although at one time recognized in quite a few states, the principle has gradually and persistently lost ground as the states, one after another, provided by statute for its elimination and enacted provisions requiring that marriages, to be legal and valid, must be performed with attendant ceremony or public record or both.

In brief, the doctrine of common law marriage is that where two indispensable requisites are present a legal marriage will result, even though there be no ceremony whatsoever. The two requisites are (1) that the parties have cohabited and (2) that the parties have held themselves out to the world as husband and wife. In many states the decisions indicate that very little "holding out" is necessary in order to constitute a holding out to the world. Thus, in a common law state, a single man and single woman might register at a hotel as husband and wife, occupy the same room together for one night, and wake up in the morning shocked to discover that they were married. It has happened.

There are valid arguments in favor of the social desirability of the recognition of the common law marriage. Perhaps the strongest argument is that children born of such a union ought not to be prejudiced in their legal rights simply because their parents were somewhat informal in the method of celebrating their marriage. On the other hand, it gradually came to be recognized that the principle of common law marriage makes it possible for many frauds to be committed, which accounts for the trend toward the requirement of more strict ceremony and publicization. The following story is a good illustration of the possibility of fraud in such cases, although fortunately in this case, by a trick of fate, justice was ultimately done. At the time this incident occurred, New Jersey recognized a common law marriage but has since by statute invalidated such common law marriages.

One day a frail looking woman dropped into the office to consult me in connection with the possible estate of her son, who had recently died in Bayonne, New Jersey. The woman turned out to be a Mrs. Hannah Brown, a widow of some eighty-odd years of age, who lived in the town of Corinth. Her son, Hubert, had left Vermont about twenty years earlier and found employment in Bayonne as a carpenter and handyman for the Standard Oil Company at very modest wages. From these modest wages he had been able to send intermittent remittances home to his mother, which, together with a few dollars she made from keeping chickens, was sufficient for her to eke out a very skimpy existence.

She had received word that her son, while working about

123

the plant where he was employed, had fallen from the roof and died without recovering consciousness. As far as she knew, he had left no will. At that time he was nearly sixty years of age. It was generally understood that he had left a small bank account of a few hundred dollars, representing his savings, and Mrs. Brown came seeking advice in connection with the method to be employed to settle his estate and get possession of the small sum of money, which would mean a great deal to her. So far as any of the family or friends of the deceased knew, he had never married. The matter appeared to be, on first impression, a simple routine matter of minor importance and simply involved the necessary statutory steps in New Jersey to appoint an administrator to settle the claims, if any, against the estate of the deceased, and to recover by decree any balance remaining, to which Mrs. Hannah Brown, the mother, would be, under the law of New Jersey, the sole heir. Arrangements were made with a local firm of attorneys, Roberts & Roberts, to handle the routine legal matters incident to settlement of the estate, and the matter was proceeding without incident or interest until a letter was received from the local attorneys in Bayonne, which indicated that this was a case of more than passing interest.

After having taken steps to procure the appointment of a New Jersey bank to act as administrator, a search of the room in which the deceased had lived for a great many years disclosed a large number of government bonds and other securities concealed in the closet. This in and of itself was a surprising development, for no one in the family suspected that the deceased had any property of any consequence. The securities totaled approximately $100,000. To this day no one knows the source of these funds, but presumably they were the result of careful investment of some portion of his modest wages. But even more surprising was the information that one Pearlstein, a Bayonne lawyer, on behalf of a woman who called herself Mrs. Brown, had filed a petition in the probate court asking that the administration granted to the New Jersey bank be canceled and that the administration be granted to the applicant. The basis for the application was the allegation that she was the legal wife of the deceased. This information was something of a shock to Mrs. Hannah Brown, because of both the unexpected existence of a sizable estate and the unsuspected existence of a wife. Careful inquiry both in Vermont and in New Jersey determined that none of Brown's relatives or friends had ever heard of this woman or of any marriage. If the claims of this woman, or any other claiming to be Hubert's wife, were true, a substantial portion of the estate would go to the wife.

Accordingly, it seemed desirable to take a trip to Bayonne, New Jersey, to make further investigation into the situation. An interview was arranged with the attorney who was acting for the claimant wife. At the interview the attorney was asked to display a copy of the marriage record between the claimant and the deceased. The attorney in reply stated that there was no marriage record, that his client was the common law wife of the deceased. It was his claim that the parties had cohabited on various occasions over a considerable period of time and that the deceased had, on many occasions, introduced this woman as his wife. If these facts were true, it was sufficient basis upon which a court might adjudicate that a common law marriage had been undertaken by the parties.

Investigation at the rooming house where the deceased had lived for many years disclosed that such a woman had frequently spent the night with the deceased and had oftentimes come down there to clean his rooms in the daytime when the deceased was not there. Evidence also indicated that on many of these visits the parties had prepared a meal and shared it.

Inquiry developed that the woman had quite definitely had a checkered career. We found that she was currently known as "Mrs. Smith," which suggested certain lines of inquiry. Following these lines led rather quickly to the discovery of a court record disclosing that she was at this very time receiving a monthly allowance of twenty-five dollars from a certain army officer by the name of Smith, pursuant to an order granted by the court on her petition for nonsupport, which was still pending in the New Jersey courts. In her petition she had alleged that she was the legal wife of Smith. The record of a ceremonial marriage between her and Smith was procured, and, armed with a copy of this record, we again called on Mr. Pearlstein, the attorney for the purported wife, and produced the copy of the record for his inspection. We expected him to be surprised and dismayed. He was neither. He told us that he knew all about the existence of this record.

"How do you expect to establish that she is the wife of Brown if she is the wife of Smith?" we asked.

"Because the marriage to Smith was invalid," he said. "It was invalid because at the time of the Smith marriage she was then married to a man by the name of French who was still living, and of course being then married to French she could not contract a legal marriage to Smith."

"Yes," we said, "but if she was not married to Smith then she was the wife of French and in either case having a husband she could not become the legal common law wife of Brown."

"Oh, no," said Pearlstein, "French was living at the time of the Smith marriage, which makes the marriage invalid, but, after the Smith marriage was performed and before she met Brown, French died. She never lived with Smith after the date of French's death so that makes the Smith marriage invalid but the marriage to Brown was valid because she was then unmarried and free to enter into marriage." He produced a record of French's death to support his statement. By this time we had a definite feeling akin to riding on a merry-go-round.

On the surface this situation seemed possible and, if true, Pearlstein's legal position was unassailable. Still, we could not escape the feeling that there was something fishy about the case. For that reason we decided to employ a professional detective to make an investigation into the history of this reputed wife. Accordingly, we made arrangements with one Sullivan, a detective from Jersey City, for carrying on such an investigation, and I returned to Barre, Vermont, to await further developments—with considerable interest and some apprehension. As Sullivan's reports began to come in, some interesting facts developed. Mrs. "Brown" had been married to still another man, one Hutchinson, prior to the French episode. Unfortunately, however, it was learned that this newly discovered husband had also died previous to the so-called Brown marriage.

But, while our investigator established the fact that the date of the Hutchinson marriage was prior to the date of the French marriage, and also the fact that Hutchinson died prior to the date alleged as the date of the common law marriage to Brown, he had been unable to determine exactly when Hutchinson died or whether that death occurred prior to the French marriage or prior to the Smith marriage. This was an important fact, as will be seen.

Thus, our position was something like this. The French marriage having occurred prior to the Smith marriage and French being alive on the date of the Smith marriage, it followed that the Smith marriage was invalid when contracted and, French having died subsequent to the Smith marriage but prior to the claimed Brown marriage, then the Brown common law marriage would be valid. But, if it could be established that Hutchinson was alive on the date of the French marriage then the French marriage would be invalid and being invalid would not be an impediment to the Smith marriage, which, if valid, would in turn invalidate the asserted Brown common law marriage. But, if on the other hand, Hutchinson lived until after the dates of both the French and Smith marriages and died prior to the asserted Brown marriage, then in such case the French and Smith marriages were both invalid but the Brown marriage would be valid. So, a successful defense involved the necessity of proving either: (1) that Hutchinson died after the date of the French marriage and before the Smith marriage, or (2) that the testimony of the "wife" was false as to the circumstances of Brown's holding out the claimant to the public as his wife. Thus, the more "husbands" we found, the more difficult our problem became.

Under the New Jersey practice and procedure, there was a provision under which either party to litigation may file what are called interrogatories. These interrogatories are a series of questions that, when filed, must be answered in writing by the other party to the litigation if within his or her knowledge, unless it can be shown that the interrogatories are not material to any issue in the case. We proceeded to file an extensive list of questions for the "wife" to answer — questions designed to ascertain the nature of the facts upon which she would rely during the trial in order to prove that Brown had held out to the public that she was his wife.

The answers to these interrogatories disclosed that she would produce testimony that Brown had written to the applicant, addressing her as "Dear wife"; that he had given Christmas presents to the mother of the claimant, which were wrapped in paper addressed "To mother"; that he had paid a dentist bill for her and in the presence of the applicant had referred to her to the dentist as his wife; that he had given the claimant a wedding ring, which was engraved with the initials of Brown and the "wife," along with the words "To my wife"; that he had bought her furniture at a large retail store in Bayonne and had had the bill charged to "Mrs. Brown" and thereafter had made installment payments on the furniture account.

Obviously, if all these facts could be proved they would amount to sufficient "holding out" of the claimant as the wife of the deceased, which, added to the fact of cohabitation, was enough to establish a common law marriage, and in such case the "wife" would be entitled to take her share in the estate of the deceased. I confess that at this stage of proceedings the case did not look too good. We decided to use all our efforts to stall the actual trial as long as possible and to continue the investigation as extensively as possible.

We furnished our detective with the material elicited by way of answer to our interrogatories. By various methods known only to detectives, and to our surprise and satisfaction, he discovered a Bayonne jeweler who would testify that the ring had actually been engraved by him at the request of the "wife" *after* Brown's death. This discovery convinced us that the whole story was a concoction, although we recognized that there was just enough truth to be dangerous and to furnish a basis for appropriate coloring enough to get by in court. We then applied to the court for an order to compel the claimant to file with the court clerk the papers and documents she claimed in answer to the interrogatories to have been written by the deceased. We then employed a famous handwriting expert to make a careful examination of these documents. Through our investigator we were able to secure, unknown to the claimant, genuine samples of her handwriting.

We received further encouragement by the expert's report — in his opinion these documents were forgeries and that they had actually been written by the woman herself. We also ascertained that the dentist, who had been referred to and who was to give damaging testimony, was a brother-in-law of the applicant's lawyer. Of course, the dentist might be honest in spite of his relationship to the claimant's lawyer, but in the whole setting we thought that fact had some significance. This left the testimony of the clerk in the furniture store, as to which we were unable to find any adequate answer.

About this time Sullivan hired a new operative. She was an extremely personable young lady of about thirty-five years who had been born in Russia, a member of former Russian nobility. She was well educated and intelligent, and she possessed an abundance of poise and charm. She was employed for the purpose of making confidential contact with the "wife" in the hope that something helpful might be uncovered, although we had little idea of just what we might find in this way. She dressed herself to fit the part of a woman of the streets and ultimately called on the "wife" at her apartment in the character of a jewelry saleswoman and by exercise of her charm was able to become sufficiently friendly with the "wife" to be accepted as a regular caller. Within two weeks the friendship developed to the point where the "saleslady" was accepted as a roommate by the "wife" on a share-the-rent basis. In a short time, confidences dropped by the "wife" in this chummy atmosphere indicated that there had been yet another husband who had preceded all the husbands already referred to. But this only added to the difficulty and confusion, for an examination of the marriage records of the place mentioned by the wife as the place of marriage failed to disclose a record. Moreover, we could not establish whether this new candidate was living or dead, and apparently the wife did not know, although she obviously thought that he was dead. His name was McCormick.

The case was fast assuming the proportions of a crossword puzzle. We now had evidence of the existence at one time or another of a total of five possible husbands, legal or illegal; McCormick, Hutchinson, French, Smith, and Brown. But unless we could show a legal husband in existence at the time of the claimed common law marriage to Brown, all of this information would be useless for defense purposes. At any rate, the discovery of McCormick's probable existence added another string to our bow. If French's marriage was valid, then Smith's marriage was invalid. But if Hutchinson's death had occurred after French's marriage and if thereafter French and the "wife" had not cohabited, then French's marriage was invalid and would not be a bar to Smith's marriage, which would be valid and would be a legal bar to the claimed marriage with Brown. But if Hutchinson's marriage was valid and he was living at the date of the Smith marriage, and if Smith and the "wife" had not cohabited after the date of Hutchinson's death, then the Smith marriage would be invalid and would not be a legal bar to the claimed marriage with Brown. Moreover, if Hutchinson died prior to the French marriage, then the French marriage would be valid and the Smith marriage would be invalid, and the Brown marriage valid. The McCormick incident, however, raised a whole new set of possibilities.

If McCormick's marriage was valid and he was living at the date of the Hutchinson marriage, then the Hutchinson marriage was invalid unless the "wife" and Hutchinson cohabited after McCormick's death, if in fact he was dead. If McCormick lived until after the French marriage and then died, the French marriage would be invalid unless French and the "wife" cohabited after McCormick's death. In that event the Smith marriage would be valid unless McCormick lived until after the Smith marriage, in which case the Smith marriage would be invalid for this reason also, unless Smith and the "wife" had cohabited after McCormick's death.

By this time we were so confused that we found ourselves hoping that no more "husbands" would be unearthed, at least until we had oriented the ones we had.

The search for evidence of the date of Hutchinson's death and also for McCormick was intensified. Another operative was set to work, and he combed the states of New Jersey, New York, and Connecticut. Occasionally, fleeting bits of evidence were found of the existence of McCormick on different dates, but these were too indefinite and contradictory to be of any value. As the time for trial was approaching, it was maddening not to be able to run down the facts concerning these two husbands.

It was at this stage of the proceedings that the court ordered us on for trial. All we could do was defend the case on the basis of the testimony of the engraver and the handwriting expert, hoping by that testimony to sufficiently discredit the woman and show that she was an impostor.

The trial commenced before the chancery court, which tries contested matters of this kind in probate proceedings. My associate, Mr. Roberts, the local New Jersey lawyer, handled the examination and cross-examination of witnesses. The opening witness was the claimant, who testified in her own behalf. Her direct testimony took all of the forenoon of the first day and continued into the afternoon session. She made a fine appearance and embellished her story with plausible statements that lent color to the transaction, and it was apparent that we would have to make a pretty good job of the defense or we were licked. And then we had a stroke of

luck — just at the right time.

Directly before the woman's direct testimony was to be concluded, we received a wire from one of Sullivan's operatives from a little town up in northern New York State, saying that he had located the fugitive husband, McCormick, and asking for instructions. We wired the operative to rush McCormick to Jersey City, implying that he should take any desperate measures necessary to insure his presence, including kidnapping. This news gave us our first real glimmer of hope. If McCormick admitted his marriage to the "wife," and if there had been no divorce, that would establish him as the real husband because of his priority of position and would thus automatically eliminate Hutchinson, French, Smith, and, most important, Brown too. We had good reason to believe that there had been no divorce. Statements made by the wife to our Russian detective indicated that. But we were apprehensive as to whether McCormick would admit his marriage at all. Since we had been unable to find a marriage record, we had no way of proving it except by McCormick.

The four hours that passed until the detective arrived with McCormick were hours of anxiety and tension. In cross-examination for the remainder of the afternoon, Roberts wasted all the time he could by going over and over the ground the wife had already covered. This is, of course, ordinarily the worst kind of strategy possible in cross-examination, but we were stalling for time. The judge could not help but realize it, and his rulings became sharper and sharper as the afternoon progressed. After what seemed an age, the afternoon session finally was adjourned, with the "wife" still on the stand and the cross-examination not completed. We heaved a sigh of relief that that phase of the ordeal was over.

About two hours after adjournment the fugitive husband arrived. We had an immediate interview with him. He showed quite clearly by his actions and appearance that he was an honest but rather dumb and harmless individual. He told us that he had married the woman in Jersey City and had lived with her less than a year when they separated by mutual consent. He also admitted that he had never been divorced.

I said to him, "Why in the world didn't you answer any of the letters and telegrams which Sullivan has been sending to you? Didn't you get any of them?" He smiled and said, "Yes, I knew you were looking for me. I have been sitting at home on the steps for more than two weeks heading off the postman and telegraph boys because, you see, I have married again and *my present wife doesn't know that I have a wife living.*"

When court opened the next morning Roberts stated in a casual way to the judge that he had just a few questions more to ask of the present witness. "Very well," said the judge, "but make it snappy. You have been wasting time all the afternoon yesterday, and our patience is about exhausted."

Roberts began by asking the woman if she did not marry a man by the name of McCormick. She denied it. He asked her a series of detailed questions as to whether she did not live with him at certain definite addresses, which McCormick had supplied us with. She denied it. But it was apparent as the cross-examination proceeded along this line that she was losing some of her composure. We had arranged that McCormick should not be in the courtroom where he could be seen. We had him secluded in a room a short distance away but in the same building. It was apparent that this new line of examination had caught the attention and interest of the judge and the officers of the court, as well as the spectators. It was obvious to most of them that Roberts was laying a foundation for something of importance. And then Roberts gave me the signal to bring McCormick into the room. I shall never forget the scene that followed.

There was an air of tense expectancy. All eyes were on the witness. The woman sat in the witness chair on a raised platform, which must have been about three feet above the level of the courtroom floor. As I led McCormick into the courtroom and we walked slowly down the long aisle to a point about five or six feet in front of the witness, the judge, the attorneys, and the spectators slowly looked at us, wondering what was going to happen. The witness, however, was still, strangely, unaware of McCormick's presence. Apparently she was in a brown study concentrating on her testimony and the troublesome questions that had been fired at her, wondering if she had handled them safely.

McCormick stopped in front of the woman and looked at her. Then she raised her eyes and saw him. She didn't move, but the queerest expression came over her face — as though she just couldn't believe what she saw. She looked at McCormick for a minute or so, her eyes growing larger and larger all the time, when suddenly she flushed crimson red and then went white as a sheet. She screamed and collapsed unconscious on the floor. Pandemonium reigned in the courtroom. The judge called to an attendant to get a doctor. In a few minutes a doctor and two white-coated ambulance attendants came into the room with a stretcher and gave the witness first aid and carried her away to the hospital.

The next morning, when court convened, Pearlstein announced to the court that his client was unable to be in court because she was still in the hospital, but that he desired to discontinue the petition.

The estate was decreed to Hubert's elderly Vermont mother.

Real Contempt

In the days when justices of the peace were holding court, they served a truly useful purpose in the rural society of their day. They took care of a great volume of the minor cases, which helped to keep the dockets of the county courts within manageable proportions. But not always did they have the complete respect to which their high office as a judge entitled them.

Justice Richardson was presiding in a civil case in the town of Corinth that involved less than fifty dollars. Sometime after the case commenced, John Daniels, a friend of the defendant, appeared in the courtroom as a spectator. Before his appearance he had fortified himself with cider brandy. In fact, this had been the reason for his late arrival. Immediately, upon his arrival, it became quite evident where his sympathies in the case lay. He was not at all pleased with some of the rulings of the justice, and he began immediately to make this fact quite clear. His comments, made in a loud voice, were quite insulting to the Honorable Mr. Justice Richardson.

Once or twice Justice Richardson warned Daniels that he was out of order and admonished him to be quiet. But Daniels was in no mood to be quiet. He was there to see justice done for his friend the defendant. The comments became increasingly more aggressive and manifestly more insulting.

Finally the judge said, "Mr. Daniels, if you interrupt the proceedings again I will cite you for contempt of court."

Rising to his feet with deliberate majesty, if somewhat unsteadily, in a most insulting voice he blurted out, "Why, you damned old fool, you don't know how to make the papers."

A Gratuitous Bit
of Evidence

Jury trials have their full complement of surprises. Usually, however, these surprises do not include the gratuitous furnishing of key evidence by one party against himself. But it does happen.

During the Prohibition Era of the 1920s, Webster Miller, Esq. was the grand juror and prosecuting officer for the city of Montpelier, and I was the state's attorney and prosecuting officer for Washington County. Together we were prosecuting a case against a Montpelier householder who was a habitual offender against the liquor laws. The charge in this case was the possession and operation of an illegal still for the manufacture of intoxicating liquor. Seems incredible now, doesn't it, in the light of present social attitudes toward liquor in all its forms?

Robert Susena was counsel for the respondent. One of the principal points of his defense was that the contraption, obviously homemade, produced by the police and marked "Ex. 1" was not in fact a still as charged. It consisted of an old-fashioned galvanized tank commonly used in those days for washing clothes. Called a wash boiler. To it were attached paraphernalia necessary to produce alcohol from mash by distillation, except one minor component—a coupling for one of the pipes. The lack of this coupling finally became the key point in the case.

At the conclusion of the evidence, Robert Susena presented a passionate argument in defense of his client. With loud voice, effective gesture, and complete conviction, he arrayed the evidence and the argument to show that without the coupling the contraption wouldn't work, and therefore it wasn't a still within the meaning of the prohibiting statute. As he reached the climax of his argument he finished as follows:

"So, gentlemen of the Jury, I have shown you that this exhibit produced by the state, though looking in some respects like a still, is nothing more than a common wash boiler. It lacks the final necessary component to make the contraption capable of distillation. What is it that it lacks? Right here, gentlemen, it needs a coupling as the testimony has indicated."

Then, in the full excitement of his argument, he turned to his client seated at the counsel table and said, "Give me that coupling." The client reached into the bag on the floor at his feet and produced a coupling, which Susena with a great flourish screwed into its place.

"See, Gentlemen, this is what is missing. Without it it is not a still—with it, it is."

Verdict: "Guilty."

I don't think Susena ever understood why.

The Inns of Court

England had its famous Inns of Court. Montpelier had its counterpart. They might be called the Inns of the County Courthouse. There was some similarity. There, in the 1920s, Montpelier lawyers had formed the morning habit of congregating in the office of Joe Frattini, the county clerk, for brief periods before repairing to their offices to take up the work of the day. Joe was the genial host and unofficial presiding officer. Here, everything was grist for the mill — pending legal cases of note, recent opinions of the Supreme Court, gossip freely shared, tall tales, local news — anything. Occasionally, some profound philosophy. But always highly entertaining. For quite a few years it remained an institution. Young lawyers absorbed much about the law and the practice of it that was not in the law books. There younger lawyers listened to the dissertations of George Hunt, William Theriault, Arthur Theriault, Fred Gleason, Judge Laird, Webster Miller, and others of the old school, to their benefit and understanding of the realities of the law and its practice. It was a most effective communication medium.

But one morning the discussion seemed to concentrate on

gossip about brother lawyers. As, one by one, lawyers would leave for their offices, the remaining members would turn their attention to gossip about their departing brother – and not always to his credit. As the atmosphere thickened with this kind of exercise, Judge Laird, local municipal judge and practicing attorney, rose to his feet, took command of the floor, and said:

"Look, boys, I've got to get over to the office to make a deed – what do you say we all leave together?"

A Special Benefit

Harry Daniels, long-time resident of East Montpelier, had more "irons in the fire" than anyone of my acquaintance. He operated a lumber sawmill, dickered in real estate, loaned money at high rates of interest to those who could not qualify for bank credit, and traded in almost every commodity you could think of. He was a canny individual who rarely got bested in a trade, and when you were negotiating with him it was best if you kept yourself especially alert and your hand on your pocketbook. But he was absolutely honest, and whatever he agreed to do he would do. But he was mighty careful as to what he agreed to.

When the federal government built the flood-control dam on the Worcester Branch, the site of the dam was such that it was built right through the middle of Harry's millpond, which served as the water power for Harry's sawmill. Harry employed me to represent him before the special commission set up to hear damage claims against the government. Believing that Harry's millpond and hence his sawmill was for all practical purposes rendered valueless, I entered upon my duties with great enthusiasm. After a long trial, the award that the commission made to Harry was about half of what I had claimed. I felt badly about this.

When Harry came in to settle up with me, I expressed my great disappointment that we had not received a higher award. I told Harry that in consequence of my disappointment in the result I was going to cut my bill in half. Harry had little to say until he had drawn a check for half the bill, carefully marking it "in full of all accounts to date." I gave him a receipt, likewise marked in full payment. Zealously chewing his unlit cigar he carefully folded the receipt and put it in his wallet. Then, removing his cigar, he looked me straight in the eye and said, "Now, Deane, I don't want you to feel too badly about this. You see, actually, building that dam where they did was a big benefit."

"What do you mean?"

"Well, you see," said Harry, "my millpond was so small and it held so little water that I could only saw about six weeks in the spring when the water was high from spring run-off. Now with all that billions of gallons held back by the government dam it is going to extend the period for two or three months more as the surplus water runs off in the spring. It has to run right over my little dam—can't go anywhere else."

Suddenly I could see that was exactly the result. Why all of us—lawyers, government engineers, and the commission members—had overlooked this vital point during the trial I will never know. It was so simple. I can only speculate that it was because we became so engrossed in a battle of real estate experts on the question of the value of the mill.

Harry didn't offer to increase the check for my fee!

Look 'em in the Eye

Two of the distinguished lawyers practicing in Montpelier when I first came to the bar were Fred Laird and Edward H. Deavitt. Laird was judge of the municipal court in Montpelier as well as a practicing lawyer. It was the custom in those days for the municipal-court judges to practice law because their duties as judges did not require their full time, and, on the salaries they were paid then, it was necessary to have an additional source of income in order to live. Judge Laird's wife was the court reporter for Washington County—and one of the best. I have heard Judge Laird say more than once, "Mother and I are doing all right these days. Making twelve dollars a day. That is—she's making ten and I'm making two."

Deavitt and Laird were attorneys for the defendant in the case of *Jones* vs. *Hughes,* which had reached the Supreme Court on appeal by the defendant. Actually, their defense was not very strong and they were following a policy of dragging their heels and asking for a continuance at each successive term of court. Finally, the attorney for the plaintiff lost his patience and filed a formal motion for judgment by default because of the failure of defendant's attorneys to file their brief as required by the rules. At the next call of the docket, the motion came on for argument in open court. The court reserved decision until the matter could be discussed in chambers.

When court reconvened after luncheon recess, the chief justice announced the decision of the court. Addressing Joseph Frattini, the clerk of court, he said, "Mr. Clerk, in the case of *Jones* vs. *Hughes* you may enter the following order: The defendant will be allowed 15 more days to file his brief, on condition that the defendant's counsel shall pay to plaintiff terms of 500 dollars." "Terms" is a euphemism for a fine or penalty. Its purpose is partly to punish the offending party for delaying the process of the law and partly to compensate the other party to the litigation for expense occasioned by such dilatory tactics. In any event, 500 dollars was a rather steep figure for those days.

Frattini, the court clerk, immediately called Fred Laird and reported the order of the court. Laird's reply was immediate and emphatic. "Joe," said Laird, "you just tell that court if they're going to fine us, we're going to be there and watch 'em do it." At afternoon recess in chambers, Frattini reported to the court exactly what Laird had said.

The next morning at nine o'clock, true to his word, Fred Laird and Ed Deavitt appeared in court and took seats in the front row of the spectator's section. They did not offer to address the court. Both, in unison, stared first at one of the justices for a full sixty seconds, then, holding that laser beam of a stare, in unison they moved their eyes to the next justice and so on from justice to justice. Meanwhile the court was listening to arguments in the case being heard. This tableau went on for twenty minutes or so, during which time the spectators, mostly lawyers, began to catch on to what was going on. This brought an increasing number of smiles and snickers until most of the spectators were tittering but trying to hide it as best they could. It was obvious, too, that the justices were having difficulty avoiding the eyes of the two attorneys. As the embarrassment mounted, the chief justice was seen to lean over and whisper to each of the justices. Whereupon the chief justice interrupted the case on trial and addressed the clerk.

"Mr. Clerk, in the case of *Jones* vs. *Hughes* you may enter the following amended order. Terms of 500 dollars imposed this morning upon attorneys for the defense is reduced to 200 dollars." Then, addressing the attorney whose argument had been interrupted, the chief said, "You may proceed."

Without a word Laird and Deavitt arose with great dignity and marched side by side up the middle aisle of the courtroom to the exit door. Just before they reached the door Laird was seen to turn to Deavitt and in a voice clearly heard throughout the courtroom he said, "There, Ed, b'God I told you so."

Turnabout Is Fair Play

Judge Rowell, later to be a Supreme Court justice, was holding court in Orange County when he was a superior judge. As I have mentioned previously, superior judges are elected by the legislature. Judge Rowell was a stern taskmaster who expected everyone to live up to the highest standards.

Eli Sprague was the clerk of Orange County Court. He doubled in brass in two other jobs. He was the janitor for the courthouse and also a popular member of the House of Representatives in the legislature. He had been elected so many times that by reason of seniority he served as chairman of one of the most important committees in the House and served as a member of several other committees. He was a most influential legislator.

Rowell's patience had been nearly exhausted. Eli was a very poor janitor. He was also known to imbibe spirits rather liberally — a practice the judge abhorred. His performance at this term of court had been far below the exacting standards of the judge, both as a janitor and as an imbiber.

One day when the judge could stand it no longer, he called Eli into chambers. "Eli," said the judge, "it is only fair to tell

148

you that I'm quite dissatisfied with your performance and conduct at this term. Everything in this room is filthy—even the spittoons have not been emptied. You're late in the morning and sometimes late after noon recess. Besides, it is obvious that you drink too much, and it is well known that you have been drunk several times. I'm warning you that things cannot go on like this. I won't stand for it. You know, don't you, that the court appoints the county clerk. We can appoint a new clerk."

"Yes, Your Honor," replied Eli, "I know that. But you do know, Judge, don't you, that the legislature elects the superior judges. We can select a new judge."

How to Make a Living

Many of our early Vermont tourists wondered how Vermont farmers could make a living on their small, rocky, hilly farms. Some still do. One of these was Gordon Beck, who lived in the midst of some of Iowa's level, richest land where corn was said to grow twenty feet high. Touring Vermont, he stopped to chat with one of our good farmers who lived on a hilly, rocky farm.

"Tell me, Mr. Smith, how much is Vermont farmland like yours worth per acre?"

"Oh — average — maybe 20 dollars an acre."

"That's amazing. Why in Iowa where I live the average price of farmland runs over 500 dollars an acre," said Beck.

"Yes, I've heard that," said the farmer.

"But how do you make a living on land like that?"

"Oh, we sell our milk, raise a few pigs and chickens, and work a little for the neighbors. But mostly we live on the interest we get on our Iowa farm mortgages."

In a Manner of Speaking

Lots of words have been written over the years about Vermonters—what they are, what they look like, how they act, and how they differ from the rest of the world. But all these attempts, I fear, have been fruitless. I have never seen a satisfactory description of what constitutes a Vermonter. I know I couldn't write one myself, even though I have lived among Vermonters all my life, and am proud to be one, too. In a way, I guess Vermonters are like Morgan horses. Easy to recognize but difficult to describe. But though I couldn't describe one, I can usually recognize one if he was born during or before the early 1900s, and particularly if he had a farm background. The best way to recognize a Vermonter is to get to know a few. And listen to them talk. A sort of indirectness that manages nevertheless to hit the bull's-eye. Here are a few examples.

"Mose" Bowen, for example, was for many years a resident of East Corinth, a tall, distinguished man, widely known throughout the state for successfully operating a bobbin mill in his hometown. You would recognize him as a Vermonter by his countenance and by his way of speaking.

While flying in a small plane over some of the largest desert areas of Arizona with his good friend Jack Hill, Mose looked down at the vast, uninhabited expanse of desert and commented, "Golly, Jack, there's an awful lot of world down there they don't use."

And on another occasion while visiting New York City with his friend, Mose stood gazing up at one of the tallest skyscrapers in the city and said, "Jack, there's a lot of brick in this village ain't there?"

Brad Thomas, formerly a vice-president of the People's National Bank of Barre, was another long-time friend. He, like Mose, was a true Vermonter, and both were ardent horsemen and shared their horse activities when both spent their winters in Tucson, Arizona. Mose used to transport his two saddle horses back and forth between Tucson and East Corinth by a trailer hitched behind his car. Since these trips took about two weeks each way and accommodations for feed and care of horses overnight were a real problem, Mose decided to have a new custom-made trailer manufactured for him by a Fort Worth, Texas, trailer manufacturer; the trailer would provide living quarters for humans in the front and space for the two horses in the rear, with only a partition between. In this way Mose and his wife could be with the horses and personally care for them night and day throughout the trip. Mose picked up his new trailer and tried it out by bringing his horses back to East Corinth in the spring. Arriving home, he telephoned his friend Brad and invited him to come over to East Corinth for dinner and see his new trailer. Brad accepted and was shortly given a chance to inspect the trailer, which he did thoroughly both inside and out, maintaining his characteristic noncommittal Vermont countenance throughout. He made no response whatever. Finally Mose, whose pride in his new trailer had led him to expect a more enthusiastic response, could stand it no longer.

"Well, Brad, what do you think of it?"

"Mose," said Brad speaking slowly and thoughtfully and still with his poker face, "I would think you would be afraid of the smell."

Whereupon Mose, equally poker faced, replied, "Oh no, Brad. You see, I have a special clause in the contract with the manufacturer that if the smell bothers the horses he has to build it over."

Calm Down

For me by far the most difficult part of jury trials was the hours of waiting for the jury to report on their deliberations. Naturally, the more important the case, the more acute was the waiting. I suspect that a majority of lawyers react this way. But not all. Some have a temperament that permits them to relax completely once their job has been done.

J. Ward Carver, my partner, and one of Vermont's greatest jury lawyers of his day, was one of those. We had finished the trial of a murder case that was a difficult one at best. We had been waiting in the lawyers' room for several hours while the jury deliberated. I was walking up and down the room in an agony of uncertainty and concern, wondering if we had done everything possible for our client. I turned to Carver and said:

"Ward, do you suppose it might have been better if we hadn't used that Scott witness at all?"

"Judge," said Carver (he used to call me "Judge"), "sit down and relax. Tain't you that's going to be hung."

An Attractive Nuisance

For another instance of the compelling manner of speaking of a true Vermonter, I am indebted to George Cook, formerly a senator from Rutland County and later U.S. district attorney for the district of Vermont. He served several terms and by 1963 had been made chairman of the Judiciary Committee. Jim Oakes of Brattleboro was a member of that session as a senator from Windham County. Jim later was an outstanding attorney general for the state of Vermont and is now serving as a member of the U.S. Circuit Court of Appeals for the Second Circuit. He had come to the Senate as a spokesman for "plaintiff's legislation." At this session, Jim, along with support from the plaintiff's segment of the Vermont Bar Association, sought to enact into law the "Attractive Nuisance Doctrine," which holds the landowner to a strict liability in many jurisdictions against claims of children injured by an instrumentality on the land to which they would normally be attracted as children and which were inherently dangerous.

Jim wanted the Senate Judiciary Committee to introduce the bill for adoption of the doctrine. He solicited support from Senator Cook, who refused. Cook said, "I believe in your bill but it won't pass. It has been tried before, and it is just something the Farm Bureau won't tolerate. I don't want to waste my time on a hopeless cause."

A few weeks later Jim came back to Senator Cook and again sought his support. Jim said he had discussed his proposed bill with "all the lady senators [Senators Keeler, Stoddard, and Ward] as well as several other senators, and there is no opposition." Jim also said, "Now we have John Boylan's bill in committee and it attempts to liberalize the use of land for hunters. My bill is a logical corollary. I would like to have the Judiciary Committee add my bill [the Attractive Nuisance Doctrine] to John Boylan's bill." Senator Cook agreed, and eventually the bill was so amended. Jim was particularly pleased because, as he said, "I not only have all the lady senators but the Fish and Game people who want the Boylan Bill." The Judiciary Committee agreed that Jim should report the bill with the amendment on behalf of the committee, giving it his full scholarly treatment, of which he was eminently capable.

The bill came up for second reading one afternoon in 1963 with all senators present except Sen. George Morse of Danville. Jim explained the bill and the amendment at length in a most scholarly fashion. Without ceremony, the amendment and the bill passed to third reading by unanimous voice vote of all twenty-nine senators. Jim came up to Senator Cook in the afternoon wearing a satisfied smile and remarked that he was glad that Senator Cook's concern had been unfounded.

The afternoon of the following day the bill, which now included the Attractive Nuisance Doctrine, came up for third reading and for passage. The question was put by the presiding officer—"Shall the bill pass?" Cook looked over at Senator Oakes. He was smiling with approval, waiting to hear a unanimous "yea" vote. But right then a voice was heard to address the presiding officer.

"Mr. President," it was the voice of Senator Morse! And Keith Wallace, the president of the Vermont Farm Bureau was sitting right behind him.

"Mr. President, I regret to say that I wasn't here yesterday. I should have been, but I had to go to the annual meeting of our Danville Cemetery Association. If I had been here I would have asked for the privilege of interrogating Senator Oakes on his amendment, which I understand passed unanimously."

Senator Oakes rose immediately and assured Senator Morse he would be glad to answer any questions. To which Senator Morse replied:

"Senator Oakes, I'm a bit interested in how your amendment will affect the fahmah. I don't really understand these lawyer words "attractive nuisance," but can you tell me the effect it would have on an example I will give you. You know, I have been a fahmah up in Danville all my life. I have always loved fahming and everything connected with it. Course I have two sons—they are grown men now—but they grew up on this fahm in the 1920s and '30s and I really loved those yeahs, and thought then they would always be on the fahm with me. Course World War II came along, my sons grew to manhood and took up other followings after the wah.

"But back in the 1930s—when my boys were hardly in their teens, they built a tree house high up in a big oak tree behind the house. It took them all summah to do and I must say they had a great time doing it.

"Course—as I said—my boys are grown up and gone now. I'm on the fahm alone now with my memories. You know, Senatah—this tree house they built way up in that tree more than 25 years ago is still up there. I know the boahds are rotten—and I guess you would call it a hazahd—even a nuisance. But you see—that tree house still gives me a lot of pleasuh. Some days, when I am feeling a bit low, I look out the kitchen windah and across the ground to that old oak tree, and then visually I climb my way up into that tree house. Why—some days I really see those little fellers up there still having so much fun—just like they did when they were young and we were all togethah.

"So, Senatah Oakes, I guess my question is: if some strange boy came along now, took it into his head to explore that tree house in my back yahd, and got seriously hurt by falling through a rotten boahd, could he sue me for damages under your bill, and could the law take my fahm?"

Senator Oakes turned several shades of red but answered firmly, "Senator Morse, that could happen."

"I see," said Senator Morse. "Well, Mr. President—I guess I don't like this bill after all 'cause it seems to hurt the fahmah. I'm going to have to vote "no," and I ask for a roll-call vote."

The roll was called: Morse 29, Oakes 1. Once again was discovered the political muscle of the Farm Bureau and the oratorical mastery of a truly great Vermonter.

The Letter of the Law

Homer Skeels, one of Vermont's distinguished trial lawyers, practiced in Ludlow with the firm of Stickney, Sargent and Skeels. A situation arose in which it was necessary to seek an emergency order to be signed by a justice of the Vermont Supreme Court. Skeels called the chief justice, George Powers, and made an appointment to meet the chief at his home in Morrisville the next day, which was Saturday. Those who practiced during any of the time of Judge Powers's long tenure will remember him well. Tall, distinguished, with a ruddy complexion and white hair, he was a dignified and handsome man who in every way looked the part of a Supreme Court judge. A great scholar, too. His Supreme Court opinions were gems of scholarly erudition and pleasing style.

When Homer arrived at the chief's home, he rang the doorbell expecting to find the judge on the ground floor. For some time there was no answer. Homer kept ringing. Finally he heard the judge's voice from above.

"Is that you, Homer?"

Homer answered that it was, and the Judge explained, "I'm in the attic and I want you to come up and help me."

Homer made his way up to the attic on the third floor and there found the judge searching the contents of an antique trunk.

"Well, it isn't here," said the judge. "Let's look in the other trunk." As he opened the second trunk, the judge turned to Homer and said, "You see, Homer, it's this way. My doctor ordered me to take a spoonful of whiskey before lunch and another before supper. And no more. Now I do not want to disobey his instructions. It occurred to me, however, that when I was a small boy I remember my mother feeding me medicine with a very large silver spoon. That's what I'm looking for."

The search continued and was rewarded with success. Homer and the judge together did a careful measurement and were both delighted to find that the antique silver spoon contained three full *tablespoons*.

Thus the judge interpreted, and applied, the doctor's instructions in the same meticulous manner in which he wrote his legal opinions. It must have paid off, too, because he enjoyed robust health as long as he lived.

There's Always a First Time

Paul Theriault operated a one-horse express business in Montpelier for years. One day, quite unexpectedly, his horse dropped dead in harness in the street at the corner of Main and State Streets, the very center of town.

Quickly a crowd gathered to view this unusual sight. As the chief of police joined the crowd, he turned to Paul and inquired, "Paul, what happened?"

"By Gol, I don't know, Chief. He never do dat before."

Not Qualified

George Blaisdell, an official of the state of Vermont, needed a secretary to replace the one he had employed for many years. The personnel department referred a prospect to him for consideration. After a preliminary interview, he thought the young lady's qualifications were probably satisfactory but decided to test her stenographic skills, so he asked her to take dictation. She was willing, and the dictation proceeded.

After a while, even though all seemed to be proceeding smoothly, Blaisdell paused and, looking at his applicant, he asked, "Am I too fast for you?"

"Oh, no," she replied, "but you're a little old."

Definition of a Horse Show

Vermont farmers, as a rule, are not enthusiastic supporters of horse shows. They think they are unproductive and a waste of time. One Vermont farmer expressed his view in real pungent language. I had asked him to feed my horses because I had to be away for a couple of days to judge a horse show. He graciously agreed. Then he said:

"Deane, did you ever hear my definition of a horse show?" I told him I had not but would be most interested to hear it.

"Well," he said, "it goes like this. A horse show is a place where the horses show their asses and the asses show their horses and you have to have judges to tell them apart."

Virtue Described

At first blush, one would not expect cemeteries to be good sources of humor. But strangely enough, they are. Especially on the older monuments erected in the days when it was customary to try to tell a bit about the deceased in the inscription. This, of course, resulted in much longer inscriptions than are used today. Many of them tell a story—partly in the lines and partly between the lines. And studying these old inscriptions not only lets you know something of the deceased, but it helps one to understand the values of people of a bygone age.

In a Vermont cemetery that shall be unnamed is the following inscription, which does invite study:

> 5 times 5 years I lived a virtuous life,
> 9 times 5 years I lived a virtuous wife,
> Wearied at last of life, I rest.
> Born 1791   Died 1864

For those of you who do not have your computers handy, please note—*there are three years unaccounted for*!

How Not to Get the Job Done

Shortly after the enactment of enabling legislation permitting towns to increase the number on the board of selectmen from three to five members, an article appeared in the town warning designed to accomplish this purpose. It was not inserted by the selectmen. Rather, it appeared as a result of a petition circulated by a disgruntled resident intent upon changing the composition of the board to affect its philosophical and political disposition by allowing for a new and hopefully more favorable majority.

When the article came up for discussion and action at the town meeting, the originator of the petition gave an impassioned explanation of the article and its virtues and moved that the article be adopted, which action was duly seconded. There was some additional modest discussion and some questioning. When it appeared that all who desired to do so had spoken, one of the incumbent selectmen, a building contractor by trade, rose to be recognized by the chair.

"Ladies and gentlemen," he said, "if I had three men working for me and I didn't like the job they were doing I sure as hell wouldn't hire two more to help them."

This appealing and irrefutable logic resulted in the immediate and overwhelming defeat of the motion.

A Double Compliment

Johnny Sanborn was a twelve-year-old lad who lived in Chelsea. His closest friend was Georgie Lyon, a boy of the same age who was the only son of the local minister. The boys went to the same school and the same church, played together constantly, and their friendship blossomed. Mrs. Lyon, being quite conscious of this friendship, invited Johnny to Sunday dinner. This was a big event for Johnny, and he and his mother had several discussions on the forthcoming event — how he should dress, how he should act, and how to behave in general. Came the day, and Johnny carefully dressed in his Sunday best, prepared to leave for the minister's home. He was very nervous. He had never been out to dinner before as a guest and of course never at the minister's home. Johnny's mother was equally concerned, for she wanted her son to make a good impression on the minister and his wife. As he left, her final words to Johnny were, "Now remember, Johnny, as soon as dinner is over you must say something nice to Mrs. Lyon about the dinner."

Everything went smoothly during dinner, but Johnny didn't enjoy it much. He was too nervous and much too preoccupied with the central problem of what to say to Mrs. Lyon. As the meal progressed, he mentally practiced what he would say to Mrs. Lyon. He tried several approaches, but none of them quite satisfied him. He so concentrated on his problem that his responses to the conversation were often quite vague.

Finally the dinner ended. This was the moment of truth. Frantically he blurted out:

"Mrs. Lyon, that was a wonderful dinner — what there was of it."

Realizing instantly that he had made a faux pas, he corrected it by saying, "And yes, Mrs. Lyon, there was quite a lot of it — such as it was."

Fortunately, Mrs. Lyon understood boys.

That's How It All Started

Hank was a long, lanky individual over 6' 3", very thin, with fantastically long legs and arms. When he took the stand it seemed almost like a complicated engineering feat for him to compose himself and to dispose of those long gangling legs. Once seated, he slowly folded his long arms and finally came to rest in an attitude that signaled he was ready for questioning. He had been sued by one of his neighbors for assault and battery, and the case was tried in Caledonia County Court.

The claim for damages arose as the result of an incident that happened on Taplin Hill when Hank and his neighbor, Fred Parker, got into an altercation when the two met on the hill at a place in the road too narrow for them to pass without getting a bit out into the snowbanks, which still lined the road as spring was starting to break up the road. Parker claimed to have been physically assaulted by Hank.

Hank's counsel stepped up to the witness chair and prepared to begin the examination of his client. It was always good entertainment when Hank was on the stand, and the courtroom was filling up fast.

"Now, Mr. Osgood, tell the court and the jury in your

own words just what happened up there on Taplin Hill on the 15th of April."

"Well, you see, Mr. Porter," he started, "it was like this. Fred and me, we never did get along much. Kinda bad blood, you know, for quite awhile. His fault though. I woulda liked to be friends with him. He was a kind of a stinker, Mr. Porter. It was in the spring of the year you know. Kinda like in between snow and mud. I was going up Taplin Hill to see Abe Peters about sellin' me some hay. Fred was coming down. Fred had his bay mare hitched to that old Concord buggy of his. I had my gray gelding and my old buckboard. We came to a pretty steep part of the hill and it was pretty narrer. Too narrer for two wagons to pass without someone getting over enough to get a wheel into the snowbank on the sides. I kinda pulled up but Fred he just kept coming and first I knew his left wheel had hooked into my left wheel and then both of us had to stop of course.

"Fred hollered at me, 'Pull over there, Hank, and give me some room.' But I was pulling uphill and naturally it would be easier for him to pull over and easier to pull out of the bank after we got by. So I said, 'Fred, pull over yourself, you're comin downhill.' He hollered at me again, 'God damn you, Hank, I tell ye pull over there and give me room or I'll swipe you one.' He had his driving whip in his hand when he said that, and I was afraid he would and it kinda made me mad. So I said, 'The hell with you, Fred, if you wanta strike you just go ahead and strike.' So Fred he lifted his whip up high and brought it down hard and fast trying to catch me across the face. When he did that I kinda reached up my arm (and here he unfolded his great long arm that seemed to have no end, illustrating what he had started to do), and when I did, in some unaccountable fashion my fingers got all tangled up in his beard—and that's the way it all started."

Missed Opportunities

The Rev. William Browning, a recent graduate of a theological seminary and just married, was seeking his first pastorate and was being considered for a call to a small Vermont town. The pastoral committee had interviewed him and his new wife, investigated his seminary record and his lifelong background, and were agreeably impressed. As was customary in those days, he was invited to preach and give the whole of his prospective congregation an opportunity to express their opinion before consummating the final arrangements. A frightening prospect for a brand new theological graduate, I must say.

And so the Reverend Browning appeared on the stated Sunday morning prepared to do his level best and face his fate. He asked his wife to sit in the back of the church to observe and later report how the congregation seemed to be taking his first sermon.

When the ordeal was over, he and his wife stood in the vestibule of the church to shake hands with the departing congregation. When the last hand had been shaken, the Reverend turned to his wife in an agony of suspense.

"Mary," he asked, "how did I do?"

"William," she answered, "you did fine. But you missed two grand opportunities."

"I did? What were they?" inquired the Reverend breathlessly.

"Well, William, there were two places you could have stopped and you didn't."

Sympathy by Design

Trial lawyers are keenly aware of the advantage of sympathy when it can be aroused on behalf of their client. They are equally aware of how dangerous it can be when it is enjoyed by the other party. A case supported by good clear logic and legal precedent can be destroyed completely if sympathy enters too strongly into the arena. These situations happen by accident and by design, but more often by design. As a young lawyer, I learned this lesson the hard way.

On behalf of Fred McAllister I had brought an action against Albert Corrigan to recover damages for breach of a contract of sale of a horse rake. My client lived in the town of Washington, so I elected to bring the suit before Justice Hamilton, a justice of the peace. The defendant's counsel was Elwyn Scott of Barre, a long-time practitioner at the bar and an experienced trial lawyer. He promptly moved for a jury trial, which was his right and which was granted.

The case came to trial in a few weeks in the town clerk's office in the town of Washington. As the trial moved on, I was delighted to find that Justice Hamilton's rulings on the admission and exclusion of evidence were predominately in my favor. As I relished this turn of events, I can remember that Justice Hamilton seemed such a capable judge – a Daniel come to judgment. It quickly became obvious to Scott that the justice's rulings were excluding so much of his offered evidence that he could not possibly win unless something drastic were done. He proceeded to do it.

As each new ruling was made against his client, he would make a long speech in which he not only detailed the already excluded evidence but, with injured innocence, accused the justice of being prejudiced against his client. These speeches were apparently directed toward the justice but actually made for the jury and, of course, were heard by the jury. Each new ruling called for a little stronger speech with the claim of judicial prejudice getting more blatant. He was accomplishing two things by his unorthodox procedure – arousing sympathy for his client and actually getting his client's excluded evidence into the minds of the jury. Juries do not always, in fact rarely, distinguish between the evidence that the attorney offers and that which is actually received through the mouths of witnesses. This is particularly so when sympathy has found its way into the courtroom.

I began to get a bit worried. I could sense the beginning of an atmosphere of hostility toward my side of the case. While I protested loud and vigorously the improper and unorthodox tactics of my opponent, I fear I only made the situation worse by creating further emphasis.

Finally, after several hours of this kind of procedure, Scott played his trump card. The justice had just excluded a bit of evidence that I'm sure the jury felt was quite pertinent to the case. They were obviously taking Scott's bold accusations of prejudice against his client seriously. Scott arose and addressed Justice Hamilton as follows:

"Your Honor, this ridiculous performance has gone on

long enough. I am a long-time member of the bar, and I have never seen a more blatant exercise of judicial prejudice than you have exhibited here all day against my client. I am sworn to defend the interest of my client, but I cannot stand by here and watch these blatant exercises in prejudice continue. What is a court unless it's fair? My client is a poor but honest farmer. You won't even let him show his side of the case. He obviously cannot get his day in court here, and I refuse to be a party to these proceedings in which he is being cheated of his rights in such a disgusting way. It offends my respect and regard for the judicial system. I won't sit here and watch his judicial execution further." Whereupon he picked up his hat and coat and stalked majestically out of the room, in every way the perfect picture of outraged dignity.

There was stunned silence in the courtroom.

Finally, when the silence became embarrassing for everyone, Justice Hamilton directed me to proceed. I did. I tried. But I quickly learned another valuable lesson. Don't ever get yourself into a situation where the other party has no attorney present to represent him. There is no quicker way to engender sympathy for the unrepresented litigant. I struggled on for the rest of the afternoon. Justice Hamilton gave his charge to the jury, which was strongly in favor of my client, almost — but not quite — directing them to bring in a verdict for my client.

The jury retired to consider its verdict. In ten minutes they returned to report. Verdict for the defendant.

Later that evening, Elwyn Scott phoned me at home. "How did the case come out, Deane?"

"You know damn well how it came out," I said.

Whereupon he laughed with appreciation and said, "Well, you know desperate cases call for desperate measures. Don't ever forget that." And I haven't.

Fortunately for my client, justice of the peace cases were fully appealable to county court, an action I promptly took. And eventually the case was settled to the satisfaction of both parties.

A case of sympathy by design.

The Party Line

Henry Hyland lived on a farm on the main road from Washington to Chelsea. This was in those happy days of the party line. Sometimes there would be as many as half a dozen telephones on one party line. Since most of those other telephones on your party line were in the homes of neighbors, the opportunity for good communication under this system was nearly limitless. A good proportion of the times when you picked up the telephone to make a call you would hear voices indicating that the line was in use. And often you would recognize the voice of one of your neighbors. If the subject of the conversation seemed to bear promise of being interesting, you just kept listening. And of course when anyone on your party line was called, everyone on the line could hear the ring and identify who was being called. If you were lonely or for any other good reason, there was nothing to prevent you from picking up the telephone when some neighbor was being called and tuning in on the conversation. This system took the place of newspapers, radio, and television of today in transmitting news. And who is to say that, for the times, the system was not equally as efficient and reliable as the present one?

Henry Hyland had a hired man, John, whose mental processes worked well but a bit slowly. He was a good worker and a fine person and, as was often the case in those days in Vermont, became a fully integrated member of the family.

Henry and his wife and the hired man had walked down the road one evening after chores and supper to visit a neighbor. While all were sitting there in the neighbor's family room engaged in interesting conversation, the telephone rang. Three rings. That was the ring for the Hyland telephone. Neither Henry nor his wife nor his neighbors noticed the call which, it would seem, is a good illustration of the psychology of association by location. Apparently, Henry and his wife failed to recognize the ring as their own because they were not at home where they usually heard it. And the neighbors failed to recognize the ring as Hyland's because they were not accustomed to answering Hyland's ring in their own home. But John, for some reason, seemed not to be under any such psychological limitations. Recognizing the ring as the Hylands', he quietly moved to the telephone, and the following took place.

"Hello," said John.

"Is this the Hylands?"

"Yes," said John.

"Is Mrs. Hyland there?"

"No, no one to home."

Psychology and the Law

In the days when I was a short-pants, unpaid law clerk in my father's law office in Barre, it was customary for deputy sheriffs and constables to rent space in a lawyer's office because there was mutual advantage for both. The lawyers issued writs and the officers served them. Usually this space was desk space in an unused back room for which the rent was quite nominal. In those days the guardians of the law served a useful purpose in the administration of civil justice as well as criminal justice. The issuance of credit by merchants was quite common but quite unaccompanied by the safeguards we have today. The result was that these officers could earn their living or at least supplement it by serving writs of attachment and a variety of other orders of the courts, for which there were fees prescribed by statute. Lawyers came to rely on these officers of the law quite heavily in the process of collecting bills for their clients. The officers were expected to perform more than the simple service of the writs of attachment. They were expected to collect the bill, which, after all, was the purpose of the issuance of the writ. And some of them did acquire a reputation for special ability to achieve collection from deadbeats by ferreting out concealed property and in other ways not now generally employed. This was before the days of the small-claims courts or the new and perhaps enlightened laws governing collection of bills.

Bert Slayton was such an officer. He had a desk in my father's office, and I was fascinated with the many ingenious methods he used to achieve success in getting money from a recalcitrant debtor. Psychology was no small part in his bag of methods.

Will Stacy operated a one-man, one-horse express business in Barre. His principal source of income was from a contract with the United States Post Office for transporting the mail bags from the trains to the post office and vice-versa. But he supplemented his income by moving ashes, rubbish, or any material desired by the general public. His motive power was a white horse of mediocre conformation and uncertain lineage. Will loved his white horse, and the feeling seemed to be reciprocated. Will responded to the horse's needs with meticulous care and great devotion. It was a mutually happy relationship.

Will had owed the Lyon Grocery Store for groceries for over a year. Mr. Lyon lost his patience and gave the bill to my father for collection. The bill amounted to $15. After repeated requests without response, my father issued a writ of attachment and gave it to Bert Slayton for service. This was a real challenge to Slayton, for Will Stacy's property condition and propensities for avoiding payment were well known. But this only served to whet Slayton's appetite for success. He felt that his reputation as a bill collector was at stake, and he threw himself into the fray with great zeal. Stacy's only visible property was his horse, harness, and wagon, all of which were exempt from attachment by specific provision of the statutes — as was his contract with the United States government, since in those days trustee process against the government was denied.

The incident occurred in the dead of winter, when the thermometer was showing temperatures of fifteen and twenty degrees below zero. As Slayton pondered the problem in the warmth of his office, he recalled that there was a train that arrived at 4:30 p.m. that would be met by Stacy and his horse and wagon. The temperature was eighteen degrees below zero. Slayton put on his coonskin hat and coonskin coat and drove his car to the station about twenty minutes before train time and, as he expected, found Stacy and his horse and wagon there waiting. The horse was covered with a warm blanket, but it was one that had been worn, torn, and patched until it was of no commercial or market value. Slayton demanded payment, which was promptly refused. Thereupon Slayton removed the blanket from the horse and took it into his possession under the writ of attachment. Horse blankets were not mentioned in the exemption statute. Stacy vehemently protested this cruelty to his horse but to no avail. Slayton then drove away and soon came back to the station by a different route and parked his car behind the station to wait and observe developments. He well knew of Stacy's love and concern for his white horse. Shortly, Stacy could no longer stand to watch his shivering horse, which frequently turned his head and looked at Stacy with reproach in his eyes. So Stacy walked over to Sherm Parker's harness shop on Merchant Street and purchased a fine new heavy winter blanket for which he paid $15 in cash. Returning to the station, he quickly adjusted the fittings of the blanket and threw it over his shivering horse. Almost immediately Slayton appeared around the corner and removed the new horse blanket and took official possession under the writ as he had done with the old blanket. This time Stacy's language was blistering enough to raise the temperature of the surrounding air at least a decimal point. Again to no avail. As Slayton drove off, he informed

Stacy that he would be in his office for a couple of hours.

In about half an hour Stacy appeared at Slayton's office, paid the full amount of the bill and the officer's fees, and retrieved his new horse blanket and the old one as well.

Thus was justice done, Slayton's reputation preserved, and the value of psychology in the law emphatically demonstrated.

An Unintelligent Test

Professor Walters, formerly a professor at the Dartmouth College's Amos Tuck School of Business, had impressive credentials for his job. He had become a professor only after a successful career in business management. As the new president of National Life of Vermont, I had become quite impressed by his combination of experience and knowledge on both the theoretical and actual side of business management. Thinking it would be helpful to all the officers at National Life who had senior responsibilities in supervision, I engaged him to give a course of lectures at National Life, one each month to a group of thirty selected officers.

One of his lectures he opened as follows: "Today I am going to speak to you on the subject of tolerance in management. But before I do, and in order to properly introduce the subject, I would like to give you all an intelligence test. Is there anyone here who is unwilling to take an intelligence test?" I doubt if there were any in the group that were happy about taking an intelligence test, but under the circumstances it was not easy to refuse. So we all sat mute trying to look as though there was nothing we wanted more in this world than to take an intelligence test in public.

"Fine," said the professor, "it's quite simple. You will be handed a printed form with a list of questions. The questions will be answered in two ways — some by simple Yes or No and others by underlining one word from a short list of potential answers. You will be given twelve minutes to finish the job. This Big Ben alarm clock I have here will be set to go off in twelve minutes after I give the signal to begin. Then I will put on the blackboard the correct answer to each question and you will score yourself by simply counting the number of correct answers. Then you will pass in your paper with the score clearly shown but with no signature or name, and I will write the different scores on the blackboard."

The test proceeded: we received our question forms, the signal was given to begin, and after twelve frantic minutes the alarm went off. Professor Walters gave us the correct answers, and we dutifully scored ourselves and passed in our papers. The professor quickly correlated the results.

"Now first let me say that I have seen this test given many times in business institutions across the country. It is a fairly common test. The average score for American business executives is 24." Then he chalked the results up on the blackboard. They came out this way.

$$
\begin{array}{l}
8 \text{ had a score of } 37 \\
2 \quad ''\quad ''\quad ''\quad '' \ 26 \\
8 \quad ''\quad ''\quad ''\quad '' \ 22 \\
7 \quad ''\quad ''\quad ''\quad '' \ 20 \\
\underline{4} \quad ''\quad ''\quad ''\quad '' \ 18 \\
29
\end{array}
$$

I watched the recording of these results with fascination. And then waited for the last score of our thirty participants with horror. It was 14, *and it was mine!*

"Now let me tell you a little about the test. First, I don't believe in the test. For several reasons. Mainly though, the questions are divided between mathematics, English, and questions calling for imagination. Your actuaries and accountants will do well with the questions in mathematics. Those in your publicity department who do a lot of writing will do well in English. I don't know who will do well in the imaginative questions. Moreover, those who have taken an intelligence test before against time know that the trick is to go down through the whole list of questions answering the ones that you can answer right off and skip the rest. Those who have not taken such tests will do the contrary and to their disadvantage because an unanswered question counts against you just as much as a wrong answer. . . Now, having said that, I want to ask if any of you have ever seen this test before?"

None had.

"Fine," said the professor. "I want you to know that I got this test this morning from your company personnel office. It is a test that every new applicant who is applying for a job in your departments must take. And so now I ask you— *do you know what I mean by tolerance in management?"*

A True Vermonter

Many Vermonters, even today, remember with appreciation two solid Vermonters whose contribution to the life of Vermont was outstanding. Olin Gay and his brother, Leon, for many years operated a woolen mill in the town of Cavendish. Olin had represented his town as representative to the general assembly and later the county as a county senator for many years. Leon was engaged in many projects of social concern and was an able, intelligent scholar. Both of these brothers lived upward of 100 years.

Many years ago Leon, who had a special interest in history, was invited to give the principal address at the annual meeting of the Vermont Historical Society. Leon accepted and thought that it might be well to introduce a bit of humor into his talk since it was a prepared dissertation on a historical subject and a bit of humor at the outset might get better attention from his audience.

"Ladies and gentlemen," he began, "I want you to know that I am greatly pleased by the honor of being asked to give this annual address. But I have a confession to make. I doubt if I am fully qualified to do so. I know it has been customary for this organization to invite only qualified Vermonters. And as you all know, a true Vermonter is one who is the descendant of a family that have been born in Vermont for five full generations. Four generations of my family were born in Vermont, and so was I. Unfortunately, my father was not. He was born in Connecticut. That was because he was born prematurely while my mother and father were on a trip to New York City."

Leon paused for the expected laughter—not a titter or even a smile. Disappointed, he bravely turned to his prepared address and struggled through it to the end. At the conclusion of his address, the president of the society, a lady of intelligence and social distinction, graciously thanked Mr. Gay for his scholarly address and added a bit of explanation. She said:

"I would like all the members to know that when Mr. Gay was invited the program committee did know all about the strange circumstances of the birth of his father outside Vermont. But on account of the special circumstances and long record of civic contributions to the state of Vermont, we decided to overlook it."

Not a single smile greeted this explanation. Obviously, History was not to be taken lightly in those days.

Judge Bicknell

Judge Bicknell has been previously mentioned. I had a great liking for him — not only because he was a good lawyer and later a good judge, but he had those human qualities which made it possible for him to relate to all kinds and classes of people. He could and did "walk with kings — nor lose the common touch." He practiced in Windsor, Vermont. He was a strong and ardent advocate wholeheartedly dedicated to the cause of whatever client he accepted. He was active in community affairs. He was a leader in the life of the town and a much loved and respected citizen. He was the "very perfect model" of a Vermont country lawyer. He worked too hard, as did most country lawyers. Finally he wearied of the pressures and accepted an appointment as a superior-court judge at a salary far less than his annual income as a practicing lawyer.

He was a good judge. He understood the law in action, and he understood the crosscurrents of human action and reaction as they unfolded before him in the courtroom. And he understood Vermonters with whom he had lived so long. He was an easy judge for the lawyers to practice before because of his abundance of experience in trial work. He enforced the law, but it was done with understanding and with compassion.

A few examples of his personality and character will suffice.

Back in his day and mine the method of assigning superior judges to the different county terms was simple and, I believe, quite unique in this country. The superior judges met once a year at Montpelier for the purpose of making the assignments. There were two terms each year in each of fourteen counties, and six superior judges to fill those terms. Someone, years ago, had reinvented the wheel. At least they had invented a new use for it. The wheel they used was similar to the ones used in gambling establishments. The names of the judges were typed on tabs pasted on the spokes of the wheel, and the names of the different terms on the rim of the wheel. With due ceremony the chief superior judge would spin the wheel and when the wheel stopped, wherever a judge's name coincided with a term, that would be his assignment for the year.

On one of these occasions a rather heated discussion broke out between Chief Judge Moulton and Judge Bicknell. The subject at issue was the wisdom or lack of it of judges picking up hitchhikers. Judge Moulton was of the opinion that judges should not do so, and Judge Bicknell of the opinion that the virtues of doing so far outweighed the risks. As it happened, Judge Bicknell, driving his own car, left the meeting first and went up Route 2 through Burlington enroute to St. Albans to begin his next assignment. Judge Buttles, on his way home to Brandon, took the same route as far as Burlington and took with him Judge Moulton and two other judges. On the way Judge Bicknell picked up a hitchhiker in Middlesex. Shortly after passing through Waterbury, Judge Bicknell had a tire blowout. About fifteen minutes later the Buttles car with Judge Moulton and the other two judges passed the Bicknell car parked beside the road with Judge Bicknell sitting contentedly in the shade on the bank while the hitchhiker worked in the intense heat to change the Judge's blown out tire. Judge Buttles was about to stop and see if any help could be given. Judge Moulton would have none of it and insisted that they keep going. Judge Bicknell waved his cigar gaily to his associates as they drove on looking straight ahead as though they hadn't seen him.

Judge Moulton received a card a day or two later from Judge Bicknell, which read, "Now who wins the argument about picking up hitchhikers?"

Once when I was trying a case before Judge Bicknell, I had to use a twelve-year-old boy as a witness. The rule was that in the case of a minor of less than fourteen years of age, it was necessary to prove first from the mouth of the prospective witness that he or she understood the nature, meaning, and consequence of the witness oath. The court had to make a finding to that effect before the minor would be allowed to testify. I had previously talked with the boy and felt that he quite understood the situation, including the consequence, if he did not tell the truth. I was wrong. His answers were all quite inadequate. Suddenly, Judge Bicknell spoke up, "Mr. Davis, you have been long enough at the bar to know that you really have to prepare these young people. Now we will recess for twenty minutes and you take this witness out in the witness room and horseshed him." There was no pretense to Judge Bicknell.

Later, when I too was a superior judge, I was driving through St. Johnsbury on my way to Newport. I knew that Judge Bicknell was holding court in St. Johnsbury and hoped that he might be having lunch at the St. Johnsbury House. I stopped to see. Sure enough, he was there and we had lunch together and had a fine chat. When the clock said 1:15 p.m., Judge Bicknell rose and said, "Well, I must be getting back to the salt mines. We resume at 1:30."

"What have you got on the griddle this afternoon, Judge?" I asked.

"Oh, just a bunch of those boring, uncontested divorce cases. Wouldn't it be great if people would just get their divorces from Sears & Roebuck?"

Stephen Rowe Bradley

If you are driving through the main street in Westminster, Vermont, and take the trouble to look you will notice an ancient-looking, small, rectangular building. This is the law office of Stephen Rowe Bradley as it was in the late 1700s when he was practicing law in his hometown. His townsmen, in grateful recognition of his many contributions to his hometown and to the state and nation, have preserved his memory by maintaining complete, untouched and unused, the one-story frame building that housed his law office.

Bradley was one of that small handful of early Vermonters who took a leading part in the events leading up to the establishment and defense of Vermont as an independent republic, and later an independent state, against the hungry clutches of three neighboring states. He fought with the Vermont Volunteers and for a time held a high military position in that group; was chosen to represent Vermont before Congress in opposition to the claims of Massachusetts, New Hampshire, and New York; served as a judge; and later was one of the first two senators elected from Vermont when the state government of Vermont was finally achieved.

According to the history of Westminster, "He took a high position and his learning and talents were the admiration of all." Legends have a special life of their own in Vermont, and Bradley was one of those legends.

Apparently, he did not suffer fools gladly, as attested to by the following incident, for which I am indebted to Sadie Smith Kinney of Rutland, a long-time court reporter and a repository of many stories and legends concerning Vermont courts and lawyers.

Bradley, appearing in court as counsel, as was his custom, placed his broad-brimmed, high-crowned frontier hat on the floor, bottom side up. Promptly, as was her custom, Henrietta, his beloved miniature poodle and constant companion, jumped into the open crown of the hat and curled herself up to snooze until her master would be ready to leave. On this occasion the matter at issue was a technical procedural motion of minor importance. Bradley's opponent was a young lawyer, newly admitted to the bar, who apparently thought a loud voice and much bombast would make up for the weakness of his legal position. Each time his voice would reach a high pitch and volume, Henrietta would raise her head in protest and utter a yip-yip. Finally, as voice, pitch, and volume reached its highest level of the day, Henrietta could stand it no longer and jumped out of the squire's hat barking furiously. To quiet the storm and restore the dignity of the court, the squire calmly put his head down and patted Henrietta's head and remarked:

"There, there, Henrietta—one pup at a time."

The Phantom Brook

Gordon Baldwin, a former associate of mine at National Life Insurance Company, was an ardent fisherman. Before he came to Montpelier he lived in Windsor, Vermont. In the early spring, a rumor was born in Windsor that rapidly gained credence concerning the existence of a newly found brook in the environs of Windsor that was teeming with fish just waiting to be caught. This was in April, just a few weeks before the opening of fishing season on May 1. It was the talk of the town as the lovers of the sport dragged out their fishing tackle in anticipation of the coming day. Talk was everywhere—in the barber shops, supermarkets, garages, filling stations, and even before and after church, indeed anywhere two fishermen came together. Unfortunately, there were about as many descriptions of the location of this fisherman's paradise as there were communicants of the story.

Gordon, however, being an engineer and hence possessed of an orderly mind, concluded that by listening attentively to all the stories he could find and extract a common thread that would lead him by deduction to the right place. This he set out to do.

On opening day, armed with fishing tackle, a lunch, a topographical map of Windsor County, and great anticipation, he set forth early in the morning in search of this phantom brook. After searching all the forenoon and much of the afternoon without success, his spirits were drooping a bit as he found himself on a grass-covered road far from habitation and completely lost. Suddenly he came upon a dilapidated set of farm buildings. His spirits rose a bit. The farmer was busily engaged in repairing a broken fence that enclosed his barnyard. The farmer paid no attention to Gordon until he had driven the last nail. Then, noticing him, he spat a generous supply of tobacco juice and inquired,

"What can I do for you?"

Since by this time Gordon had become quite suspicious that his leg had been pulled by the rumor, he was not about to admit either that he was lost or what his true mission was.

"Oh," said Gordon, "I just wanted to inquire where does this road go?"

"Well, where do you want to go?" said the farmer.

"Oh, just anywhere."

"Well, Bub, you've arrived."

Justice Allen R. Sturtevant

There are many lawyers still living who remember Judge Sturtevant, who lived and practiced law in Middlebury, had an active and lively practice, and was an outstanding citizen in every sense — the very prototype of a Vermont country lawyer. Later he was appointed a superior judge and served for quite a few years before being appointed as a justice of the Supreme Court of Vermont. One of his outstanding characteristics was an active and engaging sense of humor. He was adept not only at appreciating humor but also at creating humor on the spur of the moment. His bearing and facial expression gave no indication of this facet of his personality. He appeared to be a very dignified person, somewhat formidable and withdrawn, partly no doubt because of an unusual weakness of vision. When not reading he wore very thick lenses, but when he was in a situation where he was required to read, as in court, he wore a pair of glasses especially made for his unusual problem that actually appeared to be a pair of small field glasses with one of the lenses much longer than the other. Both sets of glasses gave him his rather forbidding appearance.

I remember an occasion in court when he was presiding in a long, hotly contested civil case. The jury had been charged and had retired to the jury room to consider their verdict. Hours dragged on, and still no report. We were all sitting around telling stories when the judge joined us. During a dull moment a young lawyer, whose performance at this term of court had been less than brilliant and who had irritated the judge, spoke up. "Judge, I've never been appointed a master in Chancery. What do you have to do to get appointed a master in Chancery?"

Ordinarily the procedure in such cases was quite simple. On request, the judge would routinely enter with the clerk of court a short, simple record of the appointment and administer the oath to any member of the bar in good standing. But not this time.

"Well, I'll tell you what you have to do. You have to do different than you've done this term."

"Sturty," as we all called him, was presiding at a term of court in Woodstock County. The case on trial was a civil case being tried with a jury. The defendant was a woman of great poise and charm who owned a white poodle that adored his mistress and accompanied her into court each day. Usually the dog was quite content to lie under the defendant's table at the feet of his mistress making no noise or disturbance whatever. But as the dull case dragged on, the dog had apparently wearied of the proceedings. He came into the center of the well, faced the jury, and successively looked each juror in the eye, cocking his head this way and that with the most expressive gesture and facial expression. The spectacle became so amusing to the jurors that soon they were concentrating completely on the dog and paying little attention to the progress of the case, which they would soon be required to decide. The court officer was the county sheriff. He was sound asleep at his post. The judge tried in every way he could think of to catch the eye and attention of the sheriff so that the dog could be quietly removed from the courtroom. But to no avail. Finally the dog began to bark. This was too much for the judge. He rapped the bench loudly with his gavel and in a thundering voice said, "Madam, you'll have to remove your dog. If you don't, he'll wake the sheriff!"

While still in general practice in Middlebury, Sturty had received a bill from his garage man for repairs on his car. The garage man had recently purchased a new system of record keeping designed to keep account of minor items usually overlooked. He was following the system to the letter, and as a result, the bill Sturty received was quite unusual—at least for the times. There was a charge for every cotter pin, every bolt, every nut, time for each machine used in the process, and even a charge for the sandpaper used in the finishing touches. Sturty was not agreeably impressed with the new system, but he made no complaint. At the time he was representing the garage man in a complicated estate settlement in the Province of Ontario. He sat down at the typewriter, pulled out the file, and with meticulous detail carefully and patiently made up a bill for services so far rendered in the estate matter and mailed it to his friend, the garage man. Sturty included a separate item for each piece of letter paper, each piece of copy paper, and for each piece of carbon paper used and included an item for wear and tear on the typewriter and other pieces of office equipment, including the chair he sat in. A couple of days later the garage man phoned him and laughingly proclaimed, "O.K. Sturty. You win. I get the point. Let's start over."

198

A fortune teller had come to Middlebury and set up transient quarters in unoccupied space on a side street. This was a rare event for Middlebury, and there was much talk about it around town, including at the Sturtevant dinner table. Sturty was a listener only. He correctly concluded from the discussion between Mrs. Sturtevant and their daughter that the two of them would soon be visiting the new soothsayer. So he went to the fortune teller, identified himself, and told her that his wife and daughter would soon be visiting her for a session. After carefully describing Mrs. Sturtevant and his daughter, he gave the fortune teller twenty-five dollars and told her that his wife and daughter would likely come to see her soon. He also disclosed to the fortune teller a few incidents of family history that she could presumably know only through her occult powers of divination and then asked her to explain to Mrs. Sturtevant and the daughter that Sturty was suffering from a rare nervous malady and that the only way for him to recover his well-being was to be treated with the greatest consideration, sympathy, and care — that he not be crossed in any way but should be allowed to have his own way in all things and pampered in every way.

A couple of days later there was clear evidence that Mrs. Sturtevant and his daughter had had their visitation. Sturty said that he had never before been treated with such solicitude. "But," he said, "it only lasted about ten days. I wonder why. But, no matter, it was well worth the twenty-five dollars."

Sturty and his wife annually planted a garden. Sturty was only slightly interested in growing vegetables, but in flowers not at all. Mrs. Sturtevant, on the other hand, cared nothing for growing vegetables but not only loved flowers but their growing and care as well. Each year there was much discussion and controversy between them over these diametrically opposed interests. How much space for flowers, how much for vegetables, what kind of fertilizer and how much to use, what insecticides to use and who should apply them. Finally, they agreed that they would put an end to such foolish bickering. And to do so they agreed that one-half of the garden would be Mrs. Sturtevant's exclusively and Sturty would have the other half. And each would be wholly responsible for his or her half.

One morning Sturty was awakened by loud noises in the backyard. Looking out from their bedroom window he saw a tractor and equipment in the process of plowing up Mrs. Sturtevant's half but carefully avoiding touching Sturty's half. As usual, Sturty handled the situation without protest. Two days later Mrs. Sturtevant was awakened by even louder noises and looking out the window saw a large amount of equipment that she could not at the moment identify.

"Sturty," she said, "what's going on out there?"

"Oh," he said sleepily, "don't worry, that's just Fred Couillard, a contractor. He's going to cement over my half of the garden."

When the famous case of "in re Wilbur" was heard in the Vermont Supreme Court, I had my first chance to function as a judge of that court. The case involved the interpretation of the last will and testament of James B. Wilbur. A sizable sum of money was at stake and was of great importance to the University of Vermont. At the time the statute provided that if a Supreme Court justice should be disqualified in a particular case, one of the judges of the Superior Court should be picked to take his place and function in his stead. Sturty and I were both superior-court judges at the time. Justice Moulton disqualified himself on the ground of conflict of interest because he was a trustee of the State Congregational Church

Society, which was one of the legatees under the will, and Justice Powers disqualified himself because he was a trustee of the University of Vermont, the principal party in interest. Sturty was picked to replace Justice Moulton, and I was picked to replace Chief Justice Powers.

As we met in the Supreme Court chambers on the day in question, preparing to enter the courtroom to listen to the arguments of counsel, Justice Powers was helping me on with my robe of office and Justice Moulton was doing the same for Sturty. Much loose banter was being tossed around. Quite seriously, however, Justice Moulton said to Sturty, "Now, Sturty, when you start up those three steps to ascend the bench be sure and pick up your skirt this way, otherwise you may step on it and make a most undignified entrance."

Sturty quickly replied, "Judge Moulton, I've learned a great deal of useful knowledge from you over the years, but I never expected to learn from you how to pick up a skirt."

As we waited for the bell to ring, I said to Sturty, "Sturty, how do you think it happened that two undistinguished judges like you and I should be picked to replace two such eminent jurists as Justice Powers and Justice Moulton?"

"Oh, that's simple," said Sturty, "we were the only two judges on the superior court that had neither any education or religion."

The Jumping Horse Story

In Vermont, in the horse and buggy days, there was a well defined and well understood standard of conduct relating to horse trades. It differed a bit, indeed more than a bit, from what was considered fair play in other trades. Outspoken falsity of the spoken word was, of course, not tolerated. Either party to the horse trade was held strictly accountable for an intentional false statement. But in order to be beyond the pale, the actual spoken words must be shown to be literally false. Even actual and intentional deceit was all right unless the words were literally false. Consequently honest double talk became a highly developed art.

Self-reliance in a horse trade meant that a man was supposed to be able to look out for himself. Else he shouldn't be trading horses. He was supposed to understand that the other party would put one over on him if possible. If one were so naïve or ignorant as to allow himself to be deceived, it was thought better to let him suffer the consequences of his ignorance that he might by sad experience grow in wisdom and stature and thus be better prepared and more self-reliant come another day. No wonder then that the quality of suspicion was

202

so highly developed in those who were members of the great brotherhood of horsemen.

The following story concerns a horse trade that did almost but not quite come off. It was between two horsemen who were long time friends. The other party was Newlin B. Wildes, now of Pomfret, Vermont, who was for many years an advertising executive, a well-recognized author, and more importantly an accomplished and skillful horseman. We both felt that we were sufficiently experienced to look after ourselves in a horse trade.

But I will let Newly tell the story in his own way:

"Horsemen, whether from New England, Vermont, or elsewhere in these United States, are generally quite recognizable people. There is ordinarily a certain aroma about them, depending on the time of day. It may be an equine mist or saddle soap and leather, or bourbon whiskey, wet tweeds or even more earthy stable odors.

But the characteristics of a horseman from New England in general and Vermont in particular are greatly sharpened when the sale or the purchase of a horse is involved. That is an entirely different ball game.

It is my considered and well-researched opinion that Vermonters under these conditions are sharper than the point of a brand new pencil. Vermonters are born and trained that way. They are not used to paying much for anything. And when it comes to selling something — watch out. Not that they are dishonest. Perish the thought. (Did you ever meet a dishonest Vermonter? Don't answer that.)

But to get away from these cruder aspects of the horse world and into a rare atmosphere, let us consider a horse sale in which I and one of Vermont's leading figures were involved. Here was a horse operation on a sublimely high plane. Almost ethereal.

At the time some years ago, I was deeply involved in an advertising business in Boston and New York. During as many nights and weekends as possible I was writing short stories for the *Ladies Home Journal,* the *Saturday Evening Post,* and so on, frequently about horses. The rest of my time was devoted to working with a string of cross country horses that we as a family owned, fox hunted, and showed around New England.

Most of the good work on these animals was done by my wife and my two daughters, all excellent horsewomen. Occasionally they tolerated my so-called helping hand. I was allowed to gallop the hunters at 5 a.m. on a nearby turf track and to fox hunt twice a week. My opinion was often given, seldom requested. My daughters enjoyed showing in hunting classes, which I could never understand. Probably they liked the blue ribbons. Be that as it may, we had our farm in Pomfret, Vermont, took the string there every summer, really legged the horses up on those hills, and showed the country circuit.

In the course of these activities, I met a man named Charles Crane. Charles was a short, unemotional pipe smoker who had been head of a foreign news bureau, finally settling for a public relations job with a large Vermont insurance company. He also wrote books, one of which was, I believe, entitled *Let Me Show You Vermont.* Fine book.

I was in Charles's office looking at the soles of his shoes propped on his desk and trying to breathe in the atmosphere created by the Old Ropey brand of pipe tobacco he preferred. Charles said, "You're a horseman, aren't you? Most people up here are cow men. But we do have one horseman in the company. Name of Deane Davis. Know him?"

I said that I had been spared that pleasure. "Come on," Charles said. He led the way down corridors and up stairs and through broom closets (this was the old building) and finally through several doors and secretaries into a huge book-lined room, quiet as a cathedral, with a desk larger than Rhode Island.

"Deane Davis," Charles said, indicating the man behind the desk. We shook hands. Deane was, and is, a big heavy-shouldered man, craggy, lined face, very keen eyes. Hell, you've seen his picture a million times. He has since been president of that insurance company, twice governor of Vermont, and the epitome of Mr. Republican.

That afternoon he admitted to being a Morgan horse man, and I told him that such a thing was possible to live down and that thoroughbreds and hunters were my dish of tea. This got us off to a rocky start, but Deane finally asked me if I would bring our horses up to his Barre show. This I eventually did, not once but frequently, and we had wonderful times although the evenings were always a slight blur.

My daughters won some ribbons there, and Deane and Charles came down to our Pomfret farm and we saw each other at various horse shows and other events around the state. And then one evening, my farm telephone rang.

"Newly," Deane said, "I know you are primarily interested in hunters, but your daughters seem to like to show open jumpers when they are offered a ride, and I thought you might be interested in something I've just come across."

I should have been warned. I should have hung up. "What is it?" I asked. There was a slight pause.

"It's an open horse," Deane said, "open jumper that has, I think, tremendous potential. Tremendous. And," his voice could not have dropped more than one conspiratorial key, "he can be bought right. Really right." I hesitated. Not for long.

"How come all this miracle?" There was another pause.

"Well," Deane said, "this friend of mine got involved in liquidating a string of horses, part of a school and camp deal, and well, he doesn't know too much about horses so he got me to sort of advise him. I saw this particular horse and he caught my eye, so I took him as my fee, part of it."

"Where is this horse?" I asked. I was hooked. Open jumpers were a popular type with the show crowd and considerably in demand. They were not ridden as 3-day horses are now. They were brought up to the jump tight on the bit, and then let go to leap off their hocks. I never thought it was a particularly pretty exhibition, but that was where the money was and I was not averse to making a buck. It helped pay for the hay and grain, and a profit was always a nice feeling.

"He's at my stable in Barre," Deane said. "Why don't you come up Saturday?"

Did Napoleon hesitate before Waterloo? Did Dewey hesitate before Truman? My bride and I went up on Saturday. But before that, I did one relatively intelligent thing. And I do so few. I went to Woodstock to see Fergy.

Fergy, Scotsman, seamed, always pleasant, state of Mainer, was running the Woodstock Inn Stables at the time. I had had a hand, a major one, in bringing him from Boston to Vermont. I had known him for years, bought a dozen horses from him, and he was as honest as any of the similes you can think of. Also he knew about every move in the horse business before it was even being considered. At the time he was on the wagon.

"Fergy," I said, "what dispersal sales, camps, schools and like that, have been happening recently?"

Fergy said he didn't know, but he could find out. "What did you have in mind, especially?" he wanted to know.

"I have in mind," I said, "a jumping horse that Deane Davis took as part of his fee. I want to know about the horse and what Deane paid for it, roughly." Fergy said he would call me. He did. Friday night.

"Brown horse," he said, "from the North Camp and School stable. Nothing much except this one horse. Understand it went on the books for under one hundred."

I thanked Fergy, told him that so and so wanted a quiet trail horse. Fergy said he had just the horse. He always did. We were even.

Deane and my bride and I had a nice lunch in Montpelier on Saturday and then drove on to Deane's Barre farm. Dick McAvoy was there. Dick usually is when something is going on in the horse world. He brought out this horse, all tacked up. It wasn't the most handsome animal I had ever seen. Bit long in the back, bit ewe in the neck, goose rumped, but a tremendous length from the hock up and a long, long stride. Nobody said anything.

Deane got on the horse, warmed it up for a while, and then galloped it up a short stretch of paved road. It seemed sound. Then he trotted it up to a four-foot-six bar way, and the horse popped it off its hocks without even hesitating. Then he let it gallop, loose rein, around a big field, collected it a little and then headed it for a good five-six gate. It cleared the gate by a foot, dropped its head and began to eat grass. Dick McAvoy wandered over and picked up each of its feet.

"Homely thing," I said to Deane finally. "How much?"

Deane didn't appear to be hearing me. We walked over and sat on a bench by the stable door. Alone. "Five hundred," he said.

I started to swear, then restrained myself. "Listen," I said, "be reasonable. I expect you to make a profit. Naturally. But, good Lord, not four or five hundred per cent. You haven't had the horse more than 10 days. You've got no board on it. I'll bet you didn't pay over $100.

Deane considered the distant mountains. "You know," he said finally in his best judicial manner (and that is very impressive), "I think this horse has the potential to be a really great open horse. That's my opinion. A really outstanding performer. I think he may be a steal at five hundred."

"Think what he was at one hundred!" I blurted. Deane ignored me. After a while he wandered over and ran a hand over the brown horse. Eventually I followed him.

"I'll give you two fifty," I said.

Deane continued to examine the horse. When he was satisfied about something, he straightened. "Five hundred," he said, "and a great opportunity."

I went over and got into my car. My wife followed me. Deane did not. I fully expected him to. I fussed with the dash and the glove compartment. I started the motor. Deane was absorbed in discussing something with Dick McAvoy.

"Goodbye," I called. "Thanks for lunch." Deane waved amiably. We drove on home.

"He'll call me in a day or so," I said to my bride, "you wait and see."

We waited, but we did not see. No phone call. I began to question whether I had been too smart. If the horse was that good—and the prices open horses were bringing. But I was stubborn. Then we went to a show down in the southern part of the state. Everyone was there. Including, to my amazement and dismay, the brown horse. He was entered in the name of one Woody Dubose, a pro whom I knew. Specialized in open horses. I looked Woody up.

We discussed this and that, and then I said, "See you have a new brown horse. I think that's the one I looked at in Barre. Belonged to Deane Davis."

Woody grinned. He was a nice guy. My daughters had ridden some of his horses for him. "Yep," he said, "I heard you'd been up there." There was a bit of silence. I knew what I wanted to find out, but those things take approaching.

Finally I said, "I might have taken a chance on the horse, but, well, I thought $700 was too much."

I watched Woody, seeing if he was going for the bait. He smiled back at me. Didn't say a word. He just grinned. I never did find out what he paid for the horse. Damn these Vermonters.

Woody went on showing the brown horse around Vermont, then into Connecticut and finally, I was told, into New York, Pennsylvania, and the big time. I sort of lost track of the thing then, and it was around the first of the year that I received an envelope in my Boston office marked "Personal."

In it was a newspaper clipping from a New Jersey paper. "So and So Stables," it said, naming a big semi-pro outfit, "has announced the purchase of the brown gelding Top Rail from Woodrow Dubose of Chester, Vermont. Rumored price ten thousand dollars."

There was nothing else in the envelope. But the post mark was Barre."

So, there's the story. All true. Oh, except for a detail here and there. Like for instance where I got the 14-year-old gelding Top Rail. Actually he was one of the horses in the stable at Norwich University, a military college in Northfield, Vermont. The horses were there on lease from the U.S. Government breeding station at Front Royal, Virginia. When the U.S. Army finally made the decision to eliminate horses and mechanize the cavalry, all the Front Royal horses were sold including those at Norwich. They were sold to the highest bidders after the horses were advertised and written bids were filed with the government — seven copies of each bid. I looked over the thirty horses in the Norwich stable, watched them ridden, worked, and jumped, and picked out seven that I thought were the best of the lot. I only wanted one, but decided to bid $70 each on seven of them in the hope of surely getting one. I can still remember the tedious chore of making out those 49 copies—seven bids, seven copies each—all in Government Englisheze.

To my surprise, three weeks later I received a telegram from Washington informing me that I was the high bidder on all seven.

Since Newly had been irked for these many years that he could not find out how much Woody Dubois paid me for Top Rail, I think now it's only fair to tell him.

It was $500 Newly, exactly what I offered him to you for.

But the real point of this story remains to be told. It is this. Never let suspicion overcome your trust in a friend. All I was doing was trying to do my friend Newly a favor. Unhappily, he had been so long in the horse business that suspicion was stronger than trust.